Lock Down Publications and Ca$h Presents

Beautiful Lies and Ugly Truths

By J-Blunt

First Edition October 2023

Printed in the United States of America

Lock Down Publications
P.O. Box 944
Stockbridge, GA 30281
www.lockdownpublications.com

Like our page on Facebook: Lock Down Publications
www.facebook.com/lockdownpublications.ldp

Stay Connected with Us!

Text LOCKDOWN to 22828 to stay up-to-date with new
releases, sneak peaks, contests and more…
Or CLICK HERE to sign up.
Like our page on Facebook:
Lock Down Publications: Facebook
Join Lock Down Publications/The New Era Reading Group
Visit our website:
www.lockdownpublications.com
Follow us on Instagram:
Lock Down Publications: Instagram
Email Us: We want to hear from you!

Chapter 1

Robert

I made eye contact with her as soon as she walked through the door. The bar was dimly lit and we were about fifty feet away, but even through the distance I could see the sparkle in her eyes. They twinkled like the little star. I wanted her. Her type was my weakness. And by her type, I meant fine. Exotic. No other woman in the bar could shine in her light. They were matches. She was a forest fire.

She wasn't that tall. Maybe 5'1". Her skin was the color of a ripe peach and she had long, dark, curly hair that showed mixed ethnicity. Some combination of Latin and black was my guess. She was dressed in a beige dinner jacket, designer jeans with tears in the knees, and a pair of black heels. She looked like her name should be Eve.

She was with a tall, mocha skin woman that wore her hair in the short choppy do made famous by Halle Berry. She wore a skintight silver dress that barely came to mid-thigh and did a poor job covering her crazy curves. Reminded me of every thirst trap on Instagram. And had she not been with Eve, she would've gotten my attention as easily as she had captured that of all the men in the room with a beating heart. But no one was getting my attention tonight. Only Eve.

"I see you, dawg!" My boy Vito slurred in a heavy Tennessee accent, his gold teeth shinning in the bar's dim lighting. "Church boy wanna take a ride on the wild side!" He laughed, flipping a floundering dreadlock over his shoulder.

"Nah, it ain't like that. I'm just admiring God's gift to man," I said, justifying my lingering stare.

4

"I'mma have to use that one." Junior smirked, giving me a glossy-eyed stare. He was buzzing good. The stupid grin on his face told me that he was past his limit.

"That wasn't a line, bro. That was the truth." I smiled, taking a sip from the bottle of Miller High Life.

"Who said anything about it being a line? What, you feeling guilty about something?" He asked, showing the dentist-whitened smile that he swore would jumpstart the modeling career that lasted all of two weeks.

"I'm not guilty of nothing but having good taste. That woman is fine. I looked. No crime in that."

"You right. The crime should be the way her friend wearing that dress. Dayum!" Junior said, rubbing a hand with the grain of his brushed waves and licking his lips. He was the definition of a pretty boy. Light skin from his biracial background, always dressed in the latest fashion, and mostly clean shaven except for a neatly trimmed mustache and beard.

"Quit actin' soft, Rob. Both of 'em fine. God ain't gon' trip, nigga. Go shoot yo' shot," Mike chimed in, speaking his mind like he always did. Unapologetically.

I looked down the bar and seen a smirk spreading across his battle-scarred face. The combination of weed and liquor had him going. The thing about Mike was, although he was a good friend, I loved and hated him. I loved the loyalty he displayed. Mike was the kind of friend that would take on the world on your behalf. But I hated that he didn't have a filter. He said what was on his mind and never bit his tongue. Growing up, his mouth got us into lots of fights.

"Nah, Mike. It ain't like that. I'm staying celibate until I find the right one."

He looked at me like I was blowing his high and then ran a hand through his short, uncombed afro. "Rob, listen to me, my nigga. God made females for us. *Made them for us*! How you gon' give up on them? It's like slappin' God in the face by not gittin' no booty."

"Amen!" Vito agreed, waving a hand in the air like he was at church.

Mike raised his voice. "God made booty for man to slap! Rub! And squeeze!"

"Amen!" Vito echoed.

"And he made them all shapes and sizes!"

"Amen! You betta tell it, boy!" Junior joined in.

"He made them round! Plump! Big and juicy! And for those who like pancakes, he made white girls!"

"Amen, brotha! Preach!" Vito cheered.

"Hallelujah! I think I feel the spirit up in here!" Junior added, fanning himself.

"And God told man, ah! I said, He told man, ah! He told man to *tap that ass*!" Mike cried out in a singsong, high pitched voice like a Baptist preacher.

We all burst out laughing. The people around the bar looked at us like we were crazy, but we didn't care. We were kicking it. These were my boys. My family.

"Man, y'all tripping. I ain't gave up on women or booty. I'm just waiting for the right one. I'm tired of all the drama these females can bring. Tired of the lies. Tired of the monotony. Drink, new woman, new problem. Drink, new woman, new problem. I'm tired of all the problems," I explained.

"I feel you, Rob, but celibacy? C'mon, man," Junior said looking at me like being celibate hurt. "I'm the only one with a kid and I want a family one day. But I can't go without sex for too long. And how long it's been for you?"

"A year and some change."

"Too damn long!" Vito cut in.

"Now, Rob, you know you my nigga, right?" Mike asked. "We go back what, fifteen years?"

"Seventeen," I corrected. Of my three friends, I had known Mike the longest. Since we were twelve.

6

"Yeah. Seventeen. And since I knew you, have I ever lied to you?"

"Nah, not that I can think of."

"And I ain't lyin' right now when I tell you that celibate shit ain't natural!"

"It is natural," I defended. "That's what God intended. Man is supposed to be celibate until he gets married."

"But this ain't 400 BC. This 2023. We done had black presidents n-shit. Shit has changed. Plus, how you gon' know if you wanna keep her unless you hit it first? You won't buy a car without test driving it, right? Why would you commit to somebody before you hit that?"

I shook my head. "Man, y'all just don't get it."

"Damn right we don't!" Vito jumped in. "And you wanna know why we don't get it? Because we get pussy!" He laughed.

"Man, I read somewhere that people who don't get off at least once a month are most likely to get cancer," Junior said with a serious face.

Mike's face went sober. "For real?"

"Straight up, brah. Said they most likely to get testicular cancer because they nuts stay full!" Junior cracked.

Mike and Vito roared like they were at a Kevin Hart show. I waved them off, taking another drink from my beer. And that's when I noticed Eve moving in my direction. I wanted to holla but I wasn't the pickup line kind of guy. I wanted our meeting to seem natural and unscripted. And now it looked like I was about to get my moment. She walked with a strut that would give any runway model in the world a run for their money. Her smile was bright, revealing pretty white teeth. Her full lips shined with gloss. I racked my brain trying to think of something to say. I wanted to make a good first impression but my mind drew blanks. Like my brain stopped working. And when I couldn't think of anything to say, I began to panic. My heart beat faster; triple-timing in my chest like I was running a race. My mouth went dry, body chilled, and palms turned clammy. When she was finally upon me, all I could do was force a weak and awkward smile. Damn.

Eve returned the sweetest smile as she breezed past. The kind of smile that could lift your spirits if you were having a bad day. And she was even prettier up close. Reminded me of the actress Lauren London. Except badder, if that was even possible. I craned my neck and watched her head towards the bathroom.

"Damn, nigga! Y'all see Rob? Nigga look like he was about to faint!" Mike laughed. "Somebody get this nigga a shot of Yak so he can relax. Knew we shouldn't have brought church boy to a bar. He don't know how to act."

I shook my head, pretending to laugh with them. If I got mad or showed emotion, they would go at me even harder. So, I sucked it up and took another sip of beer.

"Ay, bar tender! Lemmie get five shots of that Patrōn XO!" Vito called, slapping a hundred-dollar bill on the bar.

"I'm good," I protested. "I don't want no hard liquor."

"Nah, man. You too up tight," Junior said, refusing to let me off the hook. "We need you to chill. You ain't been out with us in a long time and we try'na kick it."

"For real. You in here actin' like you scared to talk to the females," Mike said. "Take these shots and loosen up, nigga."

I gave in to the peer pressure. When the bar tender lined up the shots, my boys cheered me on while I downed them. I hadn't drank hard liquor in almost a year and it burned down my throat. I quenched the fire with the rest of the beer before ordering another. Wasn't long before the liquor took effect. Time seemed to speed up and slow down at the same time. It had been a while since I got drunk and now that I was feeling the good vibes from the Patrōn, I began to question why I had stopped drinking in the first place.

"Dawg, if y'all had to choose between Oprah and Gale, who would you smash?" I slurred. After the words left my lips, I realized I was tore up. The spirits had released my inhibitions. I was saying whatever came to mind. No filter.

"Fuck kinda question is that?" Mike frowned.

"Gale. She got a ass like a horse," Vito answered.

"Oprah, nigga. She worth billions. I'll make her ass fall in love and buy Bentleys for everybody!" Junior laughed.

"I say Oprah, too. Them titties—"

"You fools tripping!" Mike cut me off. "I'm only sliding in baddies. For me to lay pipe, she gotta be a nine or better."

Vito called him out. "Mane, that's bullshit!"

"What?" Mike mugged, like he couldn't believe Vito had spoken against him.

"You heard him, nigga," I jumped in. "That's bullshit. What was o'girl name that we caught you at Junior's with? She looked like a Muppet Baby but had a body like—"

I stopped talking when I noticed Eve and her friend heading in my direction. About forty-five minutes had passed since our awkward encounter and now that I had liquid courage flowing through my body, I was about to do my thing.

"Awe shit! Church boy done went P-I-M-P on us!" Vito laughed.

I ignored my boys as I stood, blocking the women's path. Me and Eve locked eyes. Her irises were gray and the 'what is he doing' look flashed across her face. Instead of trying to think of something to say, I said the first thing that came to mind. "Watch the turtle."

She frowned. "What?"

"Watch the turtle," I repeated. "He only moves forward by sticking his neck out," I said and bust out laughing. I didn't even know why I was laughing. Maybe because I was drunk. Maybe because I knew that was corny. But I didn't care.

Eve looked confused. Then her and the friend began laughing with me. "What does that mean?"

"It's about progress. In order to elevate and move forward, sometimes we have to stick our neck out. My name is Robert. You?"

She hesitated, looking me up and down as if judging my intent. "Heaven. And this is my friend, Sandra."

I was surprised by the biblical connection to the name I gave her in my mind. "Heaven. Is that your real name?"

"Mama gave it to me."

"That's unique. Can I buy you and your friend a drink?"

"Uh, sorry, Robert but we were just about to leave."

Her words stabbed me in the heart. "I'mma be honest with you, Heaven. I've been sitting here trying to think of something to say to you since you walked in. You so beautiful that its intimidating. And now that I got the opportunity, I want to know if I could take up some of your time. I'm not try'na steal your freedom or run game but I want to get to know you a little. So would you stay just a little longer?"

Heaven was weighing my words.

"Yes, she will," Sandra answered.

Heaven cut her eyes at her friend. "Sandra, I have to go."

"Girl, did you just hear what he said? He's a good one. I can feel it. Just stay for a little while and talk to him. It's not like you have a life."

The friends had a stare down. It looked like the stare of fighters right before they threw blows. Then Heaven's stone face began to crumble. "I hate you, Sandra." She laughed. Then she turned to me. "Okay, Robert. I have a couple of minutes."

I couldn't hide my smile. "So, what are y'all drinking?"

"Nothing for me," Heaven said.

"Stop being a Debby Downer, girl. Relax. Let's enjoy ourselves," Sandra said. "How about we start off with some shots of top shelf!"

I got the bar tender's attention and ordered six shots of Patrōn XO.

"This is a bad idea." Heaven winced as the bar tender poured drinks.

Without any shame or hesitation, Sandra grabbed a shot and slammed it. "Wooo! Yeah! You don't know what you missing, girl. Here. Drink this and stop thinking."

Heaven stared at the shot glass like it was sin.

I grabbed a shot and lifted it for a toast. " You can't find out what you're drawn to until you're exposed to it. To new possibilities and a new beginning!"

The rest of the night went by in bits and pieces. I remembered being on the dance floor with Heaven. Our hands were all over each other. At some point my shirt came off and we ended up back at the bar drinking again before going back out on the floor to bump and grind. I remembered looking into her eyes and thinking how fine she was. She set my body on fire like only one other woman could. At some point we left the club together and climbed into my pearl white 1977 Chevelle on 26" chrome wheels. She laughed from the passenger seat as I drove away. And then everything went blank.

Chapter 2

Heaven

Oh my goodness! My head was hurting something fierce. It felt like there was a war going on between the left and right side of my brain. Neither side was winning but they were inflicting plenty of damage. I tried to open my eyes and quickly regretted that. A white light exploded somewhere in the front of my head, almost making me throw up. I reached a hand up to rub my head and that's when I felt the body next to me. *What the hell?*

I shot out of bed like a whale breaching the surface of the ocean for air. A streaking pain bounced from the top of my head all the way down to my feet. It hurt so bad that I wanted to scream. But I didn't want to disturb whoever was sleeping. I looked around and noticed that I was at home and the body in my bed was a he. Problem was, I didn't know who he was or how he got there.

"What the..." I mumbled, trying to remember what I did last night.

A tap on my door forced me to abandon the mental search. I had to answer the door before it opened or there was more knocking. I wasn't ready to face my bad decision yet and needed him to stay asleep as long as possible.

"Heaven?" A voice called from the hall.

I moved for the door as fast as I could, holding my breasts to stop them from flapping. And that's when I realized I was naked. "Oh my God!" I squeaked, pausing to search the dimly lit room for something to put on. Before I could cover my nakedness, the knocking started again. I glanced at the sleeping man as I abandoned my quest for clothing and raced for the door. Not waking him was more important than being seen naked. I cracked the door, trying as best as I could to conceal my body.

Ray stood in the hallway shooting daggers at me with his stare.

"Wait, honey. Give me a second to put on some clothes." I closed the door before he could respond but the disappointed look on his face said more than words. He knew I had company and didn't like it. After fumbling around in the closet, I grabbed a pink terry cloth robe and threw it on. I also put on the fakest smile that I could muster as I opened the door. Ray was waiting for me. "Good morning." I smiled, quick-stepping past him towards the bathroom.

"Man, don't g'morning me. Why you bringing niggas to our house and making fuck noises all night? I thought you was done messing with 'no good niggas'. Thought you was saving yourself for marriage. Ain't that what you said?" He scolded. Ray was my little brother. My big little brother. At fifteen, he was 6'1", 240 pounds, and wore a size 12 shoe. And he swore up and down that he was my man, father, and guardian all wrapped up in one.

I stopped to point a finger in my big little brother's face. "Don't you be cussing at me, little boy! You betta watch your mouth. You know I don't play that!"

He looked me up and down, snarling his lip. "Like I'mma listen to you. Know we gotta go to church but you wanna go out drinking and fucking."

I wanted to punch him in the mouth. "You better watch your mouth, Ray! I ain't playing. Curse at me one more time and I'ma knock the light skinned off you!" I threatened, clenching my fist.

Ray didn't say another word. Gave me the angry and disgusted look before walking away. I let out a frustrated grunt before heading to the bathroom. The encounter with him made my headache worse and I needed to hurry up and take a couple Tylenol. I had just grabbed the red and white bottle when I heard the pitter patter of small feet.

"Mommy, mommy!" Jason called, running into the bathroom followed by his twin, Mason.

"Good morning, boys."

"G'morning, mommy. Is we going to church?" Mason asked.

"Yes, we are. As soon as y'all eat and get dressed. Tell uncle Ray to make y'all some cereal."

"I want Captain Crunch!" Jason screamed as he ran from the bathroom.

"I want Fruities!" Mason called behind him.

After the twins left, I popped two pills and cupped some water in my hands to wash them down. My mind immediately went back to the man in my bed. Ray said I slept with him, but I didn't remember it. Wasn't even sure if he wore a condom. I sure hoped he did because I wasn't on the pill. I sat on the toilet to pee and think. I remembered going to the bar with Sandra. We were supposed to meet Ronald there. An hour into our wait, I realized Ronald had stood me up. I got angry and was about to leave when the man approached me. What was his name? Sandra talked me into having a drink with him. Somehow that drink turned into... Dang. I don't even remember how many drinks I had. We talked, drank, and danced. Then everything went black.

"Urrrr!" I grunted in frustration.

I knew going to that bar was a mistake. Taking Sandra was an even bigger one. I worked with her and didn't really know her that well. I took her as my wing woman because I couldn't take my friend, Reesy, to a bar. I should've left when Ronald didn't show up. Why didn't I leave? After emptying my bladder, I stood to wash my hands. When I looked at my reflection in the mirror, I felt ashamed. I had ruined five years of progress in one night. Now I had to go listen to the preacher and feel guilty all over again. "Good job, Heaven."

As I dried my hands, I thought about how I was going to get the man out of my bed. I didn't want to face him. I was scared and needed more time to think. So, I took a shower to get my thoughts together. After I finished drying off, I threw the robe back on and headed for my room. I twisted the knob as quietly as I could, not wanting to wake him. Then I thought about it. I did want to wake him. So, I bust into my room like a woman on a mission. To my surprise, he wasn't sleep. He was putting on his underwear. His back was to me, and I got a good look at his muscular butt before he slid into the black boxers.

"Whoa!" He flinched, spinning around quickly.

"I'm sorry. I didn't mean to scare you," I apologized.

I tried to remember the lines I rehearsed in the shower but had a hard time because my one night stand had the body of an Egyptian God. He was tall, lean, and muscular. Shoulders that looked sculpted by a master artist. A broad chest that I wanted to lay my head on. Powerful arms that looked like they could carry me to the moon and back. Eight pack abs. Smooth light brown skin. Low haircut. Dark eyes, a wide nose, and full lips.

"Uh, sorry about this. I just need to get dressed and I'll be outta here," he mumbled, tripping over his words as he slid into his pants.

His nervous reaction surprised me. He was acting guilty, like he did something wrong. I wasn't expecting him to behave that way and it left me speechless. So, I stood by, leaning against the door frame as he got dressed. When he bent down and picked up the condom wrapper from the floor, I looked towards the ceiling and mouthed a silent 'Thank you, Jesus!'

"I guess I'll be on my way," he mumbled, sliding into his shirt as he walked towards me.

I stepped aside, allowing him to pass. And that's when I heard the commotion.

"Mommy! Mommy! Mason trying to hit me!" Jason yelled, running full speed into my room and right into the man's legs. Mason came around the corner a moment later and tripped over Jason.

"Whoa, man! Y'all bout to kill me," the man said, bending down to help Mason up.

"What are y'all doing?" I asked, helping Jason.

"Mason tried to hit me," Jason whined.

"What did I tell y'all about fighting? Huh? Stop it. Mason, apologize to Jason."

Mason poked out his bottom lip and stared at the ground. "Sorry, brother."

"Now go back to the kitchen and finish eating."

"Kay," they mumbled before shuffling away.

"I'm sorry about that," I apologized to the man. "They are always going back and forth."

"It's cool. I know how kids are," he said, pausing like he was searching for my name. "Heaven."

Recognition flashed in his eyes. "Heaven. Right. I'm Robert. I normally don't do this but... Uh... I have to go. Can you show me the way?"

His nervousness was refreshing. "Follow me."

When I opened the front door, he stepped onto the front porch, turning back to me. "Uh, have a good day. Cute kids," he said, giving a little wave.

"Thank you. You have a good day, too."

There was an awkward pause, like he wanted to say more. "Okay. Right. Bye," he mumbled before walking away.

He was probably one of the weirdest guys I had ever met. The white, old-school car with the big shiny wheels screamed drug dealer but he acted good mannered and wholesome. Like a mamma's boy.

"That mug is tight! Ooh, look at them wheels!" Ray whistled.

16

I closed the door and headed for the kitchen.

"What happened to you being celibate?"

I turned around to face my little brother. "We're not about to discuss what I do with my body."

"You sweat me and get all up in my business when I mess up, now it's my turn. Who was that? How long you knew him? What happened to you being celibate?"

"I met him last night. I messed up and got drunk and I—"

"You got drunk!" He screamed.

"Shhh! Keep your voice down. I don't need you judging me. I know I messed up. I didn't mean to do it, but it happened. I haven't been with nobody since I had the twins. Don't try to be all up in my face because I messed up one time."

Ray gave me a long stare. I could see him weighing whether or not he should forgive me. Then he smiled. "Sorry for cursing at you. I just don't want nothing to happen to you. I never seen you talk to a dude so I kinda spazzed out when you brought dude home. Sorry."

His apology made my heart smile. "Awe! You worried about big sister? That's so cute!" I gushed, reaching out to hug him.

"C'mon, man! Stop!" He said, trying to push me away. "Teddy bears and puppies is cute. I'm a man. Say I'm handsome."

Chapter 3

Robert

I couldn't believe I was acting like a sucka!

Heaven had me stuttering and tripping over my words like a star struck twelve-year-old at a BTS concert. It was like she had a spell on me. A serious one. Wouldn't be surprised if she knew voodoo.

"Where the hell am I?" I questioned aloud as I drove down streets I had never heard of. I lived in Milwaukee my entire life and had never gotten lost. Until now.

After finding my location on my phone, it showed that I was in West Allis, a suburb outside of Milwaukee, Wisconsin. I didn't even remember driving out here. As a matter of fact, I didn't remember much of anything about last night. Didn't remember leaving the club, driving to West Allis, and I definitely didn't remember having sex with Heaven. But apparently, I did because the proof was still wrapped around my main man. I had taken sex off the menu for a reason. I wanted to get to know the woman before we lay down. Know her history. What she did for a living. Her goals. If she went to college. If she believed in God. Her outlook on life, love, and marriage. And most importantly, whether or not she was crazy! Many men had ignored the warning signs when dealing with a crazy woman because we were blinded by the sex. Got so caught up in pleasure that we missed the little things that would later become unsurmountable obstacles. Then, when we finally realized the pleasure wasn't worth the drama, it was usually too late. Some men had to pay mentally, physically, or financially when they finally distanced themselves from their bad decision, myself included. As I drove the highway, I pulled out my phones to check the messages.

My 'regular phone' had a bunch of lewd messages from my boys. I knew they would have a lot to say about last nights behavior. I talked about God, celibacy, and finding a good woman but proved I was lacking the most important ingredient to being table to practice what one preaches. Self-control. And not remembering how bad my behavior was to last night made it worse. I hoped I didn't make a fool of myself.

After throwing the phone on the passenger seat, I picked up my 'special phone'. Only one person had the number and she left so many messages that the voicemail was full. I didn't even bother listening to them. I knew what they said, and I knew what she wanted. And right now, I didn't have time for neither. I needed to get my head right, get my butt home, and get dressed for church.

I lived by myself in a single-family home in a working-class neighborhood on Milwaukee's northwest side. The wood and brick two hundred thousand dollars cape cod was my baby. I had been living there for two years and planned to have it paid off in twenty. I was able to afford the car and house thanks to my job as a welder and up and coming motivational speaker.

After parking the donk in the garage, I went right to the bathroom to flush the used condom down the toilet and shower. When I was cleaning, I went to find something to wear. Settled on black Salvatore Ferragamo jeans, a button up shirt, and a pair of Mauri gators. I stepped to the mirror to check my appearance. My brushed waves looked like the ocean, lining was crisp, goatee trimmed, and peanut butter skin shined like new money. Satisfied with my look, I sprayed on some Gucci Cologne, slipped on my Seiko watch, and hit the garage to hop in my grey 2019 Buick Regal. The Chevelle only came out on special occasions. My everyday car was a Buick.

During the drive to church, I listened to my boy James Fortune and Fiya. His music always put me in the mood to worship. I had been going to church since before I could walk. Moma made sure I was baptized when I was five. Then somewhere along the way I became a teenager and church faded into the background. I tried my hand in the streets and that turned out to be a tragedy. I lost way more than I could afford and ended up in a bad place. Somehow, I made it through the trials and got my life back on track. And now I tried to have my butt in a pew every Sunday. By the time I pulled into the church parking lot, I was in a worshipping mood. Mount Zion Baptist Church was a big state of the art building that could easily fit three thousand people. With every step I took, I could hear the choir more clearly. The thirty-member worship team sounded like angels. And the pastor was no slouch either. Reverend Bernard Wright kept us on our feet, shouting and clapping during his sermons. And I was in need of a good word. My night with Heaven had me feeling stained.

When I entered the building, I spoke to the mothers and deacons before finding a seat and listening to the choir sing a few more songs. Mother Wright took the podium next to read a scripture and pray. Next were the testimonials where members of the church got up to speak about the miracles God worked in their lives. Then finally, Reverend Wright took the podium to bring the word. The pastor was a brown skinned well-groomed man in his mid-fifties. What I liked most about him was his love for the people. He would go out of his way to help anyone. And his preaching was on point too. More of a motivational speaker than a fire and brimstone preacher, which I liked.

"Good morning, church!" He began. "If you have a Bible, please turn with me to Romans 12:1. The scripture says, 'I beseech you therefore, brethren, by the mercies of God, that you present your bodies a living sacrifice, holy, acceptable, unto God, which is your reasonable service.' "

After reading the scripture, he paused to look over the church. I avoided his eye contact. This was going to be a long service.

***

Pastor Wright's sermon echoed in my head as I walked across the parking lot towards my Buick. Our bodies were vessels that the spirit of God inhabited. We needed to keep ourselves uncontaminated to keep us in communion with God. Then Heaven popped into my head and made me feel guilty.

"Botha Johnson!"

I turned towards the voice and seen Reverend Wright headed in my direction. "What's up, Rev? That was a good word."

"Thank you, son. I say what the Lord wants me to say," he said as we shook hands. "Are you still doing motivational speaking engagements?"

"I haven't done one in about a month, but yeah. I speak when I have the opportunity."

He smiled brightly. "Good, good. I know this is kind of impromptu, but I need your help. As you know, the church is throwing a shindig at Dineen Park in about an hour and the guy I had speaking flaked on me at the last moment. We'll be entertaining about a hundred at risk youth, and I know you have a special place in your heart for the misguided. Will you give me a hand? Do some mentoring, self-esteem building, shoot a little hoops, and eat some barbeque. What do you say?"

"Well, if it wasn't for you, Rev, I wouldn't even have a platform to speak on. You gave me my first gig and I'm forever indebted. Plus, you had me at shooting hoops. How can I say no to that?"

The Reverend gave another smile, shaking my hand again. "Thank you, son. Brother Jovan and some guys from the band are coordinating the effort. Meet up with them and they'll give you the logistics."

After parting ways with my spiritual leader, I went to find brother Jovan to find out more about the event. Ten minutes later I was back in my car, listening to Lecrae and headed to the park. I had just pulled up to the stop light when my phone rang. It was Mike.

"Yeah."

"What up, my nigga?"

"Nothing. Just left church and on my way to the park to talk to some kids. Got a lil' hooping and barbecuing going on."

"Hooping and barbeque? What's the catch?" He asked. Basketball was his favorite sport and barbeque was his favorite food.

"No catch, brah. Just doing something to help the kids stay out of trouble."

"I'm on my way, nigga. What park?"

"Dineen. Right off Capitol."

"I know where that is. I'm on my way right now."

"A'ight. Holla at you in a minute."

"Wait, wait, wait nigga! Why you so in a rush to get off the phone? I wanna know what happened to that fine but booty thang you left with last night."

Images of how I reacted to Heaven this morning flashed into my head. I didn't want to tell him the truth. "Ain't nothing happen."

"Nigga, quit lying. We seen y'all stumble up outta the bar last night. That pussy was weak, huh? That's how them bad ones be. It gotta be bunk if you don't wanna talk about it. Lotta niggas probably done ran through that. Either that or you had trouble bringing yo' lil' soldier to attention!" He laughed.

I left the church riding a spiritual high but talking to Mike caused it to drop faster than an airplane with engine failure. He pulled me from my heavenly place and back down to the sinful earth. "Man, to be real, I don't even remember. I blacked out. When I woke up, I left." He didn't like my response. "What? Nigga, you serious? You blacked out? I knew I should'da got at her. Damn, Rob. You tricked off a cold piece, my nigga."

I didn't want to talk about her anymore so I rushed off the phone. "Okay, brah. I gotta go. Meet me at the park."

"A'ight, man. We gon' holla 'bout this some more when I get there. I can't believe you don't remember."

I shook my head. That was my boy, but he was good at ruining somebody's good time. But I was determined to get it back. I turned on Lecrae's song, 'Blessing' and started rapping along. Then my 'other' phone rang. Damn. I don't even know why I brought it with me. I stared at the phone on my passenger seat like it was a bomb and thought about cutting it off. But that would lead to an even bigger argument than the one looming. She had already sent a million texts and filled up the voicemail. I had to face her. So, I answered.

"Hello?"

"Oh, so you do like keeping yo' dick attached to yo' body, huh?"

"Hey to you too, Sapphire," I mumbled.

"So that's how you talk to the mother of yo' boys? What, I'm bothering you now? Why you didn't answer yo' phone last night? Where was you at? Where you at now?"

"I just left church. I'm on my way to the park to mentor some kids."

"Why you mentoring somebody else kids when you could be mentoring the boys? We ain't seen you in a week. When you comin' over? And where was you at last night?"

"What's up with all these questions? I don't got time for this right now."

Her attitude turned up a notch. "Oh, you don't got time for me now? What about the boys? You don't be sayin' that shit when I be suckin' yo' dick, do you? What bitch you wit'? You got one of them church hoes witchu?"

I shouldn't have answered the phone. "Sapphire, for the millionth time, those ain't my kids and you not my woman. I don't got time to be arguing with you. I told you I got something to do."

"C'mon, Robert!" She whined. "You know those DNA tests can be wrong. And I love you, baby. You my first love."

I wasn't trying to hear none of the senseless stuff she was spitting. "I don't got time for this right now."

"So that's how it is, Robert? Gettin' all brand new on a bitch."

"Look, I gotta go. I'ma holla at you later."

"Nigga, if you hang up this phone—"

I hung up before she could finish the threat. And for good measure, I hit the power button too.

Chapter 4

Heaven

I glanced at the clock on the dashboard as I climbed out of my sky-blue KIA Optima. 8:26AM. I needed to get in and out of the post office quickly so I could get to work and get on with my day. I walked in and was happy to find the stamp vending machine free. I ordered a row and pulled the envelope from my purse. It was addressed to Laron Landry, AKA Lay-Lay, an inmate at Waupun Correctional Institution. I felt some kind of way just popping up on him out of the blue. The fact that I was about to drop a bomb on him didn't make it any better. I wanted my letter to be well received. I had been searching for answers to my questions for almost three years. I was hoping and praying that Lay-Lay could end my quest for the truth.

After sticking a stamp on the envelope, I dropped it in the mailbox and headed to work. I was a certified nursing assistant at the Forest Park Retirement Home. I helped take care of the elderly when their families gave up on them or they were too old to take care of themselves. I'd been working there for three years and although I liked the bond I'd developed with some of the patients, and the fifteen dollars an hour plus benefits wasn't bad, I was ready to move on. I wanted better pay and a career. Being a nursing assistant for thirty or forty years wasn't the career for me. I was looking to step up and become a real nurse at a big hospital. Planned on going to school for it next semester.

When I walked in the nursing home, I smiled and greeted everyone that I passed in the halls. Most of my coworkers took me for a wholesome Christian girl that was cute and naïve as Eve. Just how I wanted it. I spent the past five years creating a newer version of myself. A bigger and better me. And that's how everyone treated me. I went to the break room to clock in and I ran into Dr Sam.

"Hey, Heaven." He smiled creepily, walking up and invading my personal space.

I took a step back to create some space between us. "Hi, Sam."

The doctor took a step forward, licking his lips while looking me from head to toe. "You know, I've never seen anyone make scrubs look as good as you do. If I was your man—"

I pulled the timecard from the slot and spun away. "Bye, Sam!"

"Why you always running from me, darling? I don't bite," he called after me.

"Gotta lot of work to do. See ya!"

After ditching Doctor Freak-n-stein, I began my rounds to check on patients. The first stop was Lorraine Coats. She was a feisty and often controversial eighty-seven-year-old white lady who spoke her mind and often reminisced about the Jim Crow era. The thing about older people was they didn't care much for being politically correct. They spoke their mind, saying what they meant. And Lorraine was the Commander in Chief of the speak your mind movement.

"Hey, Lorraine!" I smiled as I entered her room.

"Hello, Heaven. It's about time someone with a brain showed up. These people are crazy. Can you tell the other colored nurse that I prefer glucose tablets. I'm tired of being poked with needles."

My head snapped quickly in her direction. No she didn't. "I'll leave a note at the desk. But just so you know, calling a black person 'colored' isn't kosher anymore. I prefer Black or African American."

"Oh, you people are so sensitive and fickle." She laughed. "First it's negro, then colored, now Black or African American. Why does being so politically correct about the name of your race matter? I'm white. I've always been white. Why can't you be colored or black?"

I sensed the sound of an unfinished debate. "Have you been talking to Majora again?"

"Yes, I have. We talk every day. And she doesn't mind being called colored either."

"That's because she grew up being called colored. I'm only twenty-six. I grew up being called African American or Black."

She waved me off. "Like I said, you people need to make up your mind. Have you ever read 'Uncle Tom's Cabin'?"

I looked up from the medicine tray and seen that she was holding the book. "I think I read it in high school."

"Don't you think slavery saved those people in Africa? I see the commercials on TV all the time. They always look dirty and hungry. At least as slaves they had clothing and food."

I took a deep breath and did a ten count in my head, trying to calm myself so I wouldn't take the book and bust her head open. "What you see on TV isn't what happens on the entire continent. And back in slavery days, my people were fine. The country was wealthy. The land was good and the animals and food plentiful. Europeans came with guns and alcohol and the world conquering attitude and tore the country up. Problems came when we left Africa and came to America."

She stuck up her nose. "You don't have to be so sensitive, Heaven. Jeesh."

"I'm not. I'm just giving you the truth about our history. Your medication is ready. Do you need anything else?"

"I'm fine."

I walked out of Lorraine's room wearing a smile. It wasn't easy to rattle her. She normally did the rattling and it felt good to get a victory. I know it was petty, but it felt good. I walked next door and into Majora's room. The ninety-two-year-old was my favorite patient in the retirement home. She was more like a grandmother than patient and I confided and trusted in her. She was sitting in a chair by the window reading the Bible.

"Hi, Majora!"

"Good morning, Heaven. God bless you, child. How are you?" She asked, sitting the Bible down and opening her arms for a hug.

I wrapped the slender woman in an embrace. "I'm fine. How are you?"

"The Lord has blessed me with another day. Every day that I open my eyes is a blessing."

"Amen."

"Lorraine didn't get on your nerves too much, did she?" Majora asked, giving a knowing look.

"How did you know?" I laughed.

"Because she complained all night long about the other nurses and said she was going to tell you the next day."

"She did more than complained. Had the nerve to call me colored."

"Oh, don't pay her no mind. She has a good heart. She just don't got tact. Don't know when to keep her mouth closed."

"That's an understatement. But I got her good when I told her how her people messed up Africa. You should've seen her face. She didn't like that."

Majora laughed with me. "Oh, Heaven! You didn't have to do that."

"Yes, I did. And it felt good, too. How are you this morning? Do you need anything?"

"Nope. I already took my medication. I'll take a walk later. Now come sit down and talk to me. How are you and those precious little babies? Have you made progress finding their father?"

"I found another guy. He's in prison. I mailed him a letter before I came to work."

"That's good. It's progress."

"I know. But it's so humiliating. I hate having to find these men and ask for paternity tests."

"Better to do it on your own than going on Maury and putting your business out there."

"I know. But I still hate it."

"I know you do. But God won't put more on us than we can bear. Plus, those boys need their father to be cured. You have to stay vigilant to give them a chance at life."

"I know. I'm not going to give up, no matter how hard or humiliating. My kids need this, and I won't let them down. I just hate how young and stupid I was."

"That is what being young is all about. Making mistakes. Maturity comes when you learn from the mess ups. And keep praying to God for the strength to persevere. I pray for you all the time."

"Thank you so much. I sure need the prayers and support."

"No problem, baby. We all have a past. Believe that. But don't let what you've been through stop you from getting to where you're going. I know it's hard, and that's the way it's supposed to be. You have to fight to live. And a good fight don't mean you won't get bruised. It just means that you didn't let the bruises stop you from fighting on."

"Amen to that," I agreed, patting her hands. "Sorry to break up our chat, but I have to finish my rounds. I'll come back in about an hour. I wanted to talk to you about Proverbs 31."

Majora's eyes lit up. "A virtuous woman. That is a good chapter. I'll do some praying and ask God to give me His words to say to you. C'mon back now."

After leaving Majora's room, I stopped at the nurse's station to leave a write up about Lorraine's glucose tablets. I had just finished the form when Sandra walked up.

"Hey, Heaven! What's goin' on, girl?"

I thought about throwing a punch. Messing with her I got drunk and had sex with a stranger. But I couldn't put all the blame on her. It was my fault for taking her with me in the first place. I shouldn't be hanging out with a wanna be Instagram model whose definition of success was marrying a basketball player.

"Hey, girl. Lorraine is already talking out the side of her neck so be careful."

Sandra rolled her eyes. "I'ma give her old racist ass the wrong medication one day. See if she be talking all that Trump shit when her heart stop working," she joked.

I laughed. "Stop, Sandra! You wrong, girl."

"I'm just playing. She almost gone so all we gotta do is wait. I hope she get buried next to black people. But forget that old witch. What's up with that fine nigga you left the bar with? I know y'all got it poppin."

I cut my eyes at her. "Excuse me? Why you all up in mines? And what makes you think I gave him some?"

She rolled her eyes. "Oh, stop with the good girl act, Heaven. Y'all was all over each other on that dance floor. Y'all was damn near freaking in the middle of the bar. So, was it good?"

"I don't got nothing for you," I said, walking away from the nurse's station.

Sandra gave chase and walked alongside me. "Heaven, you betta stop acting like you an old lady. Girl, you twenty-six, not fifty six. And you fine. I don't get you. Why don't you want to have fun or go out? All you do is work, go home and talk about church and Jesus. What the hell is wrong with you?"

I felt a little sorry for Sandra. Her priorities were all wrong. Getting high, partying, and sleeping with random men were her ideas of living a good life and having fun. She didn't

30

understand the important things in life like family, faith, and love. Or what it meant to be a real woman. Or that modesty, self-control, and using discretion weren't bad words and were needed to make good choices. She didn't know the dark places that I'd survived and managed to crawl away from. She couldn't understand that when you were as close to death as I had once been, that every heart beat and moment above ground was a blessing to be cherished. And when I tried to tell her about it, she normally shrugged me off or pushed me away.

"I told you I don't care about that stuff. None of that is important to me. There is more to life than chasing good feelings. I'm more concerned with my kids and making sure they grow up to be good men. I'm concerned where I will spend eternity. I'm concerned about you thinking that because I don't have your type of fun that something is wrong with me. What if something is wrong with you?"

Her face went flat. "Girl, do you see the way niggas look at me. Do you see this body? This face? Nothing is wrong with me. I'm blessed. You betta ask somebody."

"I didn't say you weren't beautiful. But you are more than a pretty face and nice body. You are a woman who should love and appreciate who she is. And be thankful that you have—"

"You know what, girl? I gotta go," she cut me off. "You about to start yo' Iyanla Vanzant, Oprah Winfrey speech and I got patients to check on. Check you in a minute."

I shook my head as she spun away. Every time I spoke truth and honesty she ran. And that was sad. But whatever. I had patients to check on too. I was about to head for Anna's room when my phone began vibrating. I pulled it out and seen a text. It was from Ron.

'My bad I missed you. Let's reschedule.'

Seeing the text sent a fire through my bones. He was the reason I was in the bar. He was the reason I ran into Robert. If he would've honored our meeting, I wouldn't have broken my celibacy vow. Ooh, as soon as I got the chance, I was going to let him know what was on my mind.

Chapter 5

Robert

I walked through my front door, stopping to type in the code to disarm the alarm before hanging my coat in the closet. Then my phone rang. "Hello?"

"Hey, baby. How are you doing?"

The angelic tone coming through the phone brought an instant smile to my face. My mother was amazing. Growing up, our relationship was a tug of war like most mother son relationships. She told me to do right, I did wrong. She told me to go to school, I cut class. She told me to get a job, I sold drugs. Then tragedy struck and everyone turned their back on me except my mother. She held my hand during the storm, showing that nothing in this world was stronger than a mother's love.

"Hey, mom. I just walked in the house. How you doing?" I asked, walking to the kitchen to grab a bottle of water.

"I'm fine. Seeing what's up with you. Do you have any plans tonight?"

She was up to something. "Nah. I was probably going to chill and do some writing."

"Have you written any new songs?"

"Nothing that nobody wants to hear." I laughed.

"C'mon now, sweety. You have a gift. You need to share it with people. What's the use in having a lamp if you keep it in the closet? Don't hide your light. Let it shine."

We'd had this conversation at least a hundred times. She wanted me to go on singing shows or join a choir and show the world my talent. She believed I could become famous and get a recording contract. I wasn't sold on the idea of singing in front of people. For me, it was personal and private like a poet's poetry. It wasn't meant for everyone to see, hear, or read.

"I don't know, mom. I'm just not ready yet. Still don't feel comfortable enough to sing for nobody."

"Why not? You sing in front of me."

"You're different. You love me. You're family."

"You can't let the stage fright hold you back. You speak to crowds of children all the time. Isn't it the same thing? What's the difference between speaking to a crowd and singing to a crowd?"

" You trying to get me to sing at your church again?"

She hesitated. "If you feel comfortable, it would be nice of you to sing at Christina's son's baptism."

"I can't believe you tried to get me like that," I laughed.

She gave a you got me giggle. "Christina loves you and so does little Michael. If you sang for them, it would be such a blessing."

"As much as I love your church friend and her son, I'm going to have to decline. I'm not ready."

"Oh, well. I tried," she breathed. Then silence. I knew there was more.

"What's going on, mom? You okay?"

She let out a breath. "I wanted to go spend some time with your brother and I was hoping you would come with me."

I sat the bottle on the table way harder than I wanted, splashing water on the polished wood. My body was instantly flooded with emotions. Sorrow. Sadness. Anger. Guilt. Visions of Roger flooded my head, going from childhood to adulthood in an instant. I was transported from my kitchen into a place where time and space didn't exist. Nothing existed except Roger.

"Robert, are you there?"

My mom's voice cut through the montage, snapping me back to the kitchen. "C'mon, mom. You know how I feel about this."

"But, baby, you haven't been to see him yet. Don't you think it's about—"

"I said no!" I snapped.

I didn't mean to get so aggressive with my mom, but I couldn't help it. Talking about Roger brought out emotions that I couldn't control. Silence filled the space between us for a moment.

"I'm sorry for snapping at you, mom. I just don't want to picture him lying in the dirt."

"It's okay. I know how you feel about this. I know it hurts for you to think of him. Freddy thought that—"

"Fred can go to hell!" I exploded, not even letting her finish.

If there was one person I hated thinking about more than my brother, it was Fred. "Don't talk about your father like that, Robert. He's a complicated man, but he loves you," she defended.

"You gon' really defend him after everything he put me through?"

"It was a hard time for the family, Robert. We all said and did things that we didn't mean. And your father thinks it's about time you face Roger. You need to get past this. We all need to get past this."

I sat down at the table and fumed. The only thing Fred could do was kiss the crack of my butt right after a fresh dump. I didn't care what he thought. I hated him. He was a terrible father. But out of respect for my mother, I kept my mouth closed. I had already shown way too much disrespect to my queen.

"Do it for me, Robert. Come see your brother. Please?" She sniffled.

Hearing my mother cry made me feel like the world's biggest piece of trash. I was torn. I didn't want to go to the graveyard, but I also didn't want to hear my mom cry any more. "Okay, mama. I'll do it for you."

***

Graceland Cemetery was thirty minutes from my house. I spotted my mother's Lincoln Town Car idling by the curb outside the cemetery's huge iron gate. I parked behind the sedan, taking a look around as I cut the engine on my Regal. The cemetery looked empty and soulless. There were hundreds of headstones in different colors, sizes, and shapes. Some of the gravesites were plain and barren. Others were decorated with flowers or balloons. But no matter how many decorations people used to dress up the graves of their loved ones and no matter how pretty the grounds keepers made the grass look, I still hated being there surrounded by death.

By the time I got out of the car, my mother was already walking to my door. At fifty-four years old, my mom was still a cutey pie. To me, she was the most beautiful woman in the world. She was 5'4" with healthy curves that came from eating soul food and getting older. She had big blue eyes that were full of life, fair skin, and curly shoulder length hair. She was the daughter of a Polish woman and a Black man from Kansas. She met my father while attending college at the University of Illinois. They got married one year after graduation and moved to Milwaukee to settle down and begin their lives.

"Hey, cutey," I said affectionately, opening my arms to embrace her.

"Hey, handsome," she crooned, rubbing circles in the middle of my back while squeezing me.

"You seem like you're getting shorter," I teased.

"Or you're the Jolly Green Giant." She laughed. Then a seriousness entered her eyes. "Are you ready?"

Hearing those words and knowing that I was about to stand over a plot of earth where the yin to my yang was

36

buried caused me to get emotional. I took a deep breath and fought back the tears.

"I'm ready."

She grabbed my hand. "You'll be okay, baby. I'm here with you."

I continued to hold my mother's hand as we walked through the sea of gravestones. My body was so consumed with emotions that I didn't notice him until we were about thirty yards away. He wore a black Kangol hat, black sweater, brown slacks, and black loafers. He stood over a gravestone decorated with white roses. Even though his back was towards me, I knew the shape of him. I stopped in my tracks, yanking my hand away from my mom's.

"What the hell is he doing here?" I asked and accused.

"Please, Robert. Your father wanted us all to meet here. Give him a chance."

"He lucky I don't hit him in his mouth!" I yelled before walking away.

"Robert, don't leave!" Mom called.

I ignored her and continued walking.

"Sledge!"

I wanted to continue walking but the sound of his voice stopped me in my tracks. It packed power and authority, reminding me of when I was a child and he was the biggest, fastest, coolest, toughest man in the world. I spun around to face Fred. We held each other's stare across the distance like duelers at high noon in a Western flick.

"Let's talk," he called before spinning towards my brother's grave.

I had ill will for my father and didn't want to talk to him. I had nothing to say. Well, actually, I had a lot to say. But I knew if I said it, I would have to fight him. I looked to my mom for an answer. Her deep blue eyes reflected her want to put the family back together. My feet moved like they had a mind of their own and the next thing I knew I was standing next to my father, shoulder to shoulder. I didn't bother looking into his face because I didn't want to see his eyes. So, I focused on my brother's granite headstone. Roger Johnson 1994-2018 was engraved in the 16"x16" rock. The reminder that my twin brother was buried six feet under the dirt opened a wound in my chest. The tears came without warning, rushing from my eyes like rapid currents in a river.

My father's voice cut through the grief pouring from my soul. "I'm sorry, son.

I looked into Fred's clean shaven, dark brown face. His top lip was trembling, eyes red and rimming with tears. The pain in his eyes tore at the strong and tougher than nails image I had of him while growing up. Hearing my dad apologize and seeing him cry were miracles to anyone who knew the Johnson family. Pop was a tough man. A no nonsense disciplinarian who'd spent twenty years in the military. Even though he was sixty, he still looked like he could take on any young punk that got out of line. Big vise grip like hands, broad shoulders and a barrel chest.

"I think it's about time we let this feud die and become a family again," he said, struggling to get the words out.

I just stared at him, confused by everything that was happening around and inside of me. Coming to my brother's grave for the first time was already an emotional experience. To have the man I'd hated standing in front of me apologizing only added to the confusion. As I stared into my father's tear-stained face, I began to think about the past eight years of my life. They were the most difficult times I'd ever faced. My father abandoned me during those trial. Thinking about it renewed my anger towards him and I snapped.

"So, we supposed to act like the last eight years didn't happen? I'm supposed to act like you didn't blame me for killing 'your' son? I'm supposed to act like you didn't abandon me and treat me like a piece of shit?"

"Listen, Sledge, I said those things out of anger. I shouldn't have said them and I'm sorry. But I was hurting, son. And I was angry at you."

"And this apology is supposed to make up for all that?"

"No. But I want it to be a start. No matter what happened between us, I never stopped loving you. I—"

"That's bullshit, Fred!" I exploded. "I did five years in prison, and you never sent a single letter, didn't come to a single visit, or send a single dime. Mom was there for me. She held me down. If it wasn't for her, ain't no telling where I would be. I been out three years, and this is our first time talking. So how can you love me? I hate yo' guts, nigga. If you didn't raise me, I would'da been punched you in the mouth!"

"I deserve that." He nodded.

His reaction surprised the hell out of me. I was sure that my words would've got him fired up.

"And you can hate me all you want, but that won't change nothing. I don't want to fight you, Sledge. And if Hammer was here, he wouldn't want us fighting either."

His composed and calm demeanor took away some of my fire. "How are you going to wait eight years to try and fix this, Fred? You blamed me for everything. Do you know what it feels like to walk around with that much guilt?"

"No. And I'm sorry for putting that on you. I shouldn't have blamed you. But it was easier that way. I didn't want to acknowledge or admit that I was at fault for not trying better to reach you when you started hanging out in the street. You were going down the wrong road and Hammer was excelling. The truth is, I gave up on you before you went to prison. I gave up on you when you dropped out of school and started selling drugs. I failed you, son. And I want to make it right. I need you, Sledge."

The apology was genuine and from his heart. But my anger wouldn't let me accept it. "Well, I don't need you, Fred. I made it without you. I became the man I am today because of my hate for you. It fueled me. The reason I began speaking to kids is so they would have someone to turn to when their parents gave up on them. You the reason I go to work every day. Knowing I became a God fearing and successful man without your input fuels me, man. I don't need you. You can keep ignoring me. You can keep avoiding me when I come to the house. I'm good."

Getting eight years of pent-up aggression off my chest felt good. Like I had been cleansed. And the pained and sorrowful look that filled my father's eyes caused a satisfied grin to cross my lips. I had hurt him like he'd done me.

"I'm dying, Sledge."

The words were mumbled and barely audible, but I heard them as loud as if someone was screaming them through a bullhorn. The good feeling that I'd felt when I saw the pain in his eyes quickly vanished and a burning pain settled into the middle of my chest. It felt like I had been poked in the heart by the tip of a sword. "Wh-What?"

"I'm dying Sledge," he repeated, the truth reflecting on his face and in his eyes. "Got prostate cancer and it's spreading. Nothing the doctors can do. They gave me a year."

The tears began spilling down my face again. They were for my father. My dying father. "When did you get cancer, pop? You don't look sick. Why didn't you tell me earlier?" I asked, looking him over for signs of sickness. He looked normal. Healthy.

"We found out a couple months ago. By the time they found it, it was too late. It's aggressive, Sledge. Just a matter of time."

No words could describe what I was feeling on the inside. I was rocked to my core and just stood speechless. I couldn't believe that my father was about to die.

"Can we stop fighting, Sledge? Please, son. I need you."

I did the only thing that felt right and reached out to embrace my dying father.

Chapter 6

Heaven

After reading Lay-Lay's letter for a third time, I sat it next to my laptop and picked up the picture he sent. He was handsome in an Akon sort of way. Very dark skin that had a healthy glow. A nice build. And a platinum toothed smile. It looked like prison was doing him good. While staring at the picture, I reflected on some of the things he said in the letter. He was locked upon for being in possession of 25 grams of heroin, his second drug charge. He talked about the changes he'd made during the three years he'd been locked up and how he was ready to get out and get his 'grown man' on. He agreed to take a paternity test and hoped that he was the father of the twins because he didn't have kids but wanted some. Sounded good to me. I kind of liked the thought of having a grown man in my life. I hadn't had a man since... Forever.

For as far back as I could remember, all the men in my life were here today and gone tomorrow. I don't think I ever met one that I wanted to keep around. Well, there was one, but he wasn't a man. Physically he was an adult, but he lacked all the qualities and attributes that separated an adult male from a man. He wasn't loving, compassionate, protective, or responsible. And I was too young to realize, know, and understand all the things that made a man a man. So, I put up with him and even thought I loved him and he loved me. But I was wrong. So-so-so wrong. But that was then. My yesterday. Today I'm a new woman and I don't need a man. I love me and I got Jesus. That's enough.

But my kids did need a father. Even though Lay-Lay mentioned how he wanted to be my kids' father, I didn't get my hopes up. I had been through this before. Several times. Not to mention, my boys looked nothing like him. He had very dark skin and my boy's complexion was as light as mine. I was expecting the outcome of this test to be the same as all the rest, but somewhere in my heart I kept that small spark of hope. After tucking away the letter and picture, I went to look for my little brother. Found him in his room playing a video game. "Hey, I need you to watch the twins while I make a run."

Ray paused the game and gave me a concerned look. He was trying to be my father again. "Where you going?"

"To see a man about a bird."

He didn't like my answer. "The last time you went to see a man, you—"

"You better not say it!" I warned, clenching my fists and stepping into his room. He was talking about my one-night stand and I didn't want to hear it.

When he saw the flash of anger, he changed his tone. "Two hours."

I laughed and gave him a mocking salute. "Yes, sir, drill sergeant."

I grabbed the keys to my KIA and stepped out into the fall weather. The brisk October breeze chilled my bones and made me think about going to get a jacket. But my car was parked out front and I didn't want to waste any more time than necessary. I had a meeting and time was of the essence. I needed to take care of business and get back home. I hopped in the car, turned the heat up and listened to Lizzo while driving. Twenty minutes later the scenery changed from the land of moms in minivans to the land of the lost, also known as hood. Milwaukee. The murder Capitol of Wisconsin. Even though I was born and raised in Milwaukee and had spent most of my life in the hood, I hated going back. Hated it like rich people hated the thoughts of going broke. I changed my bad habits and destructive ways and now I wanted to stay as far away from my old life as possible. Which is why I moved to the suburbs. Now every time I went to the city was on my terms. Like today. I had to meet Ron at a Mexican restaurant on the South Side. I pulled up to the stop light across the street from Alejandro's and texted Ron the color and make of my car. I was driving through the parking lot when he texted back:

"Orange Porsche truck. You will hear me."

A few moments later I could hear bass booming as my car vibrated. An orange SUV on big chrome wheel pulled into the parking lot. Back in the day, his truck would have gotten my attention. Cars with big rims, loud music, and expensive paint jobs used to excite me like cat nip does kitty cats. But today I was a new woman on a mission for her babies so I could care less about the truck. In fact, I wished he wouldn't have driven it. It was loud and attention grabbing, and I was trying to remain low key. After he parked his street version of a monster truck a few spaces from my KIA, I climbed out to meet him. On my way to the sporty SUV, he and three friends climbed out followed by a humongous weed cloud.

"Sup, shawty? You looking good as a mu'fucka!" Ron said, grabbing his crotch and licking his lips.

He was tall, light skinned, and handsome. I gave a nervous smile, keeping my focus on him and ignoring the way his friends were looking at me. I was dressed in blue Nike's, jeans, and a white T-shirt but they ogled me like I was naked.

"Damn, she strapped!" One of them said as they headed for the restaurant.

I didn't even acknowledge his presence, hoping my body language let them know I didn't want their attention. "I thought you were coming by yourself," I said, looking up to Ron as he towered over me.

"I ain't say nothing 'bout coming by myself. You know how it is out here. Niggas a love to catch Ron-Ron slippin'. I stay with a team. Niggas want these precious stones and I ain't givin' 'em up for free," he said, flashing a smile that cost

44

enough to send Ray to college. He also wore a chain and watch that would've made most rappers envious.

"Okay. I get it. But I need to talk to you in private. It's important."

He cocked his head to the side. "What you got, shorty? I'm dyin' to know why you actin' all secretive n-shit. I hope it's some freaky shit 'cause you bad as fuck! Lookin' like Maliah in that Drake video. I betta find yo' loving!" He sang, grabbing me by the waist.

I pushed his hands away. "Stop, Ron. I'm not playing."

He took a step back and gave me a serious look. "Oh, you on some real shit? What, you got AIDS or some shit? I know you ain't 'bout to start screaming 'bout some kids 'cause you hit off me and my nigga at the same time. So, what is it?"

I didn't like the way he was talking and looking at me like I was a gold digger. For a moment I thought about telling him I had AIDS just to scare him. But this was no time for games. "I think you might be the father of my twins."

His eyes grew wide. "Fuck outta here!" He said, spitting a luggie on the ground like my news left a bad taste in his mouth.

I didn't speak. Instead, I stared at him with a straight face.

"Can't be mine. I always strap up. You betta go find anotha nigga," he said before walking away.

I grabbed his arm. "Wait. Just hear me out."

He stopped to give me a crazy look.

"I'm not a gold digger trying to pin a baby on you and take your money. I don't want nothing from you. I just need to know who my kids' father is. They are sick and need a bone marrow transplant. I'm not a match. I can support and take care of my own kids. But they need this operation. Please."

Ron-Ron gave me a long stare, trying to see if he could detect a lie. "You straight up, on some real shit?"

"I swear on my life."

He continued to give me the searching stare. I never blinked. "A'ight, shawty. What I gotta do?"

I pulled the tube with the swab in it from my pocket so fast that it looked like I knew magic. "I need a DNA sample. A mouth swab."

He took the tube, looking me up and down while licking his lips. "And what's in it for me?"

I looked at him like he was crazy. "You can do the right thing."

He laughed. "I'm just playing. I got you." He opened the tube and swabbed the inside of his cheek. "How long before I know something?"

"Couple weeks. I'll call you."

He put the swab back in the tube and handed it to me. "Twins, huh? Boys or girls? How old?"

"Five-year-old boys."

"Five-year-old boys, huh?" He repeated, smiling a little.

I took my cue to leave. "Okay, Ron. It was nice to see you. I gotta go."

"Wait, girl. Don't leave yet. Holla at me for a minute. I agreed to meet you here, thinking you tryna kick it and you surprise a nigga with a DNA test. Tell me what's goin' on with you. You gotta nigga?"

I didn't want to stay and talk. I was a mama on a mission and so far, I had completed half of it. But I also didn't want to be rude. "I don't do anything. And I don't have a man either. I'm celibate. Jesus is my lover and my Lord."

"Celibate? Jesus?" He asked, saying the words like they tasted funny.

"I'm not that girl anymore, Ron. I'm a mother and I'm happy. I just want to do what's best for my kids."

He shook his head like he couldn't believe what I was saying. "Damn, that's crazy. But I feel you. You gotta do what's best for your kids."

"I do. Well, I have to go. Gotta put my boys to bed. Take care of—"

"Red Bone! Red Bone!"

The sound of his voice sent a chill up my spine. No way! It couldn't be!

Ronald and I spun around at the same time. A middle-aged dark-skinned man was getting out of a silver Bentley. He wore a tailored olive-green suit with matching shoes. His permed shoulder length hair bounced as he strode purposefully in our direction.

"Hoe Whisperer, what's good nigga?" Ron asked, extending a hand.

"What's up, Ron-Ron? I see you found one of my gems," he said, staring at me angrily.

I was terrified out of my mind. My worst nightmare had come to life and was standing right before my eyes. I wanted to run but my feet wouldn't move.

"What? Not Heaven, pimpin'. She a good girl," Ron said, looking back and forth from me to the pimp.

"Get over here, girl. Right now! Right now, bitch!" The Hoe Whisperer demanded.

I felt hopeless and didn't know what to do. The gossipers said he moved to another state. What was he doing here? I had hoped that the next time we crossed paths, I would be stronger and able to stand up to him. But seeing him so unexpectedly proved how much I wasn't ready to face him. The only thing keeping him away was Ron standing between us. I knew that if I tried to leave and The Hoe Whisperer got me by himself, things would get ugly. So, I stood frozen behind Ron.

"Aye, she wit' me, dawg. Chill that shit," Ron said, picking up my distress.

"Nigga, this pimp bidness. Get out the way!" The Hoe Whisperer said, waving Ron off and walking towards me.

Ron grabbed his arm. The Hoe Whisperer paused, looking up at him like he'd violated a code. Tensions rose. It looked like they were about to fight. Then Ron's friends started coming from the restaurant.

"Okay. I see what it is," The Hoe Whisperer said, pedaling back away. "Gotcha goons out with you tonight, huh?"

"I told you she was wit' me, pimpin'," Ron said.

"Okay, Ron-Ron. But dig this, playa. Once a hoe, always a hoe." Then he looked at me. "I'ma see you round, Red Bone. Believe that." Then he hopped into the silver car and sped away.

"Fuck was that about? You know that nigga?" Ron asked, judging me with his eyes. All the respect he'd gained for me when I told him I was a changed and celibate woman was gone.

I couldn't take the look in his eyes or those of his friends. My feet started moving and the next thing I knew I was back in my KIA racing home.

Chapter 7

Robert

The vibrating phone pulled me from sleep. I hurried to answer it. "Hello?"

"Rob! Whatchu whispering for, nigga?" Vito asked.

"I'm sleep," I whispered, keeping my response short.

"Dawg, me and Mike on our way to yo' house right now to pick you up. We gotta stop Junior. He on his way to Madison right now. He pissed off and drunk, and I think he gotta burner."

I was no longer sleepy. "What? What happened?"

"Amber called and said her step daddy slapped her. Junior on his way to Madison to catch a case. We gotta stop him, brah. Know that nigga still got five years on parole. We almost to yo' house and—"

"Wait!" I yelled, wincing and looking to the other side of the bed when I realized how loud I was.

"What up, brah?"

I lowered my voice. "I'm, uh, not at home. I'm at mom's crib. Don't come get me. I'ma meet y'all in Madison."

"A'ight, fam. Hurry up. We gotta get to Marrissa house before he do. We can't let that nigga go back to jail."

After hanging up, I sat up in bed, staring across the dark room. I couldn't believe my luck. Why did this have to happen tonight? I was trying to remain low key and chill. But that had been ruined by the need to save a friend from destroying his life.

"Damn," I mumbled before climbing out of bed. I used the moonlight that shone through the window to find my clothes. After sliding on my shoes, I tip toed towards the door. I got it halfway open when the bedside lamp switched on.

"Where you goin', Robert?"

I spun around and locked eyes with Sapphire. She was sitting up in bed, shooting me with sleepy-eyed daggers. "Uh, that was Vito. I gotta go."

"Why didn't you tell him where you was at? You ashamed of me?"

I wanted to say, "Hell yeah!" but that would start an argument that I didn't have time for. "Nah, baby. You know it ain't like that. I was just trying to hurry up and get off the phone because I didn't want to wake you up."

She gave me the look. "Stop lying, Robert. I know you better than you know yo'self."

"I gotta go, Sapphire. I need to get to Madison before Junior do something stupid. Something happened to his daughter, and we can't let him go back to jail."

"But what about my needs? You gon' leave all of this?" She threw back the covers, revealing her birthday suit. Her body looked like it was made to please. Smooth and soft brown skin. 34 DDs with big dark areolas. Flat stomach. Small waist and wide hips that made it look like she'd been wearing a waist trainer. And she had a booty that got hundreds of likes every time she posted a back shot on Instagram. Her face was plain at best. Deep set dark brown eyes, a wide nose, and thick lips. But her beauty wasn't what kept me coming back to her bed. It was what she did in the bed. It was too much for me to resist. But I held fast. My boy needed me.

"I'ma make it up to you later. I promise," I said quickly before leaving the room.

"Check on the boys before you leave!" She called after me.

I acted like I didn't hear her, heading for the door and dashing outside like I was being chased by somebody with a pistol. Five seconds later I was in my Regal sticking the key in the ignition. I didn't even give the engine time to warm up before I pulled away from the curb. The drive to Madison was normally an hour and a half ride. I ignored the speed signs and did ninety all the way there. Saved thirty minutes. I turned onto Brown Street on Madison's north side, and spotted Vito's yellow Lexus parked in front of a black and gray two story town house. Mike and Vito were in the car with him. I searched the block for Junior's Benz as I climbed from the Regal. There was no sign of him. I walked up to the Lexus's driver's side and squatted down.

"He here?"

"Nah, not yet." Vito shook his head. "But we gon' chill for a lil' bit just in case he show up." "Y'all been up to the house yet? Anybody talk to Marrissa?"

"Yeah, we holla'd at her," Mike spoke up. "Marrissa and o'boy had a fight. The nigga hit Marrissa, not Amber. He still in there snapping out."

I shook my head. "Well, that—"

My words were cut off by tires squealing as Junior's Benz came fish tailing around the corner. The European engine revved loudly as the luxury car sped towards us. Tires squealed again when he hit the brakes and the car came to a skidding stop.

"I'ma kill this bitch ass nigga!" Junior screamed, hopping out with a black handgun.

"Chill, Junior!" I yelled, walking towards him with my palms out.

He ignored me and ran towards Marissa's house. Vito and Mike climbed from the Lexus and we chased Junior. Vito got to him first, tackling him to the ground. I jumped on top of Junior, helping to hold him down while Mike wrestled the gun away.

"Let me go, Vito! Get off me, Rob!" Junior squirmed. "I'ma kill that nigga. Let me go!"

"Chill nigga," Vito said, pinning down his arms. "You on parole, nigga. We ain't finna let you go out like that."

"Straight up, brah. We yo' boys," I added, holding down his legs.

"He didn't hit Amber, nigga. Quit whylin' out," Mike said nonchalantly.

"Junior? What are you doing here?"

We looked up and saw Marrissa staring down at us. Junior's baby mama was a Cuban cutey. She was flanked by her boyfriend and some of their neighbors.

"Did that bitch ass nigga put his hands on Amber?" Junior yelled, his neck veins bulging as he mugged his daughter's mother and her man.

"You betta watch yo' mouth, nigga. I gotcho bitch," John threatened.

John was a big 6'4" and about 250 pounds. By comparison, Junior was 5'10", 185. Even though my boy packed a lot of muscle and worked out regularly, I didn't think the fight would be fair. John was a giant compared to Junior.

"He didn't touch our daughter, Junior. You know I wouldn't allow that," Marrissa said.

"So, what the fuck is going on? Why Amber call me crying? What this bitch ass nigga do?"

"Junior, just leave. Our problems don't have anything to do with you. I can handle it."

"Get the fuck outta here with that bullshit, nigga," John spoke up. "And if you call me another bitch, we gon' have a problem."

I let go of Junior's legs and stood. I wasn't looking for problems, but I also wasn't about to let this linebacker attack my guy.

"Chill, John," Mike intervened. "Go back in the house. My nigga drunk but we got him. It's all good."

"Tell that nigga to watch his mouth. I don't care how many niggas y'all got with y'all. Can't none of you niggas fuck in mine." John barked.

This wasn't going to end well.

"Get off me so I can whoop this nigga ass!" Junior yelled, sliding from under Vito and jumping to his feet. He rushed John with clenched fists but he was drunk and his coordination was off so I was able to grab him before he threw a punch.

But John was ready to go. He tried to rush Junior but Mike stepped in and gave him a shove. "Ay, nigga, chill! We about to leave."

"Fuck that nigga and fuck you too! I'll beat both y'all asses!" John yelled, throwing a wild punch.

Mike ducked just in time. Had the punch landed, we would've been picking my boys face up off the ground.

"Well, fuck it then, nigga! You want these problems?" Mike yelled, throwing up his fists. Vito was about to jump in but I held him back. Mike and John moved to the grass and squared up. On paper, Mike was the underdog. John had him by two inches and about sixty pounds. But I had been watching Mike fight since we were kids. John was bigger and stronger but Mike was about to beat him down. My boy was hands down the best street fighter I had ever seen. Probably could've done MMA if he had taken it serious.

"Guys, stop!" Marrissa yelled, about to get between them.

"Nah, shawty," Vito said, pulling Marrissa back. "They grown men. Let them do them."

I looked at the crowd of neighbors gathering around. They looked on expectedly, wanting to see a fight. John threw the first punch. It was a wild haymaker that Mike was able to duck. The second punch smacked loudly when it landed on Mike's jaw. He stumbled and took a couple steps backward. Mike recovered and threw a flurry of punches, most of them landing in John's face. The big man let our a roar as he threw another wild punch. Mike jumped out of the way and they squared up again. I was able to get a look at John's face when they separated. Blood from his nose and lips dripped down his chin. John touched a hand to his face to check the damage. Rage flashed in his eyes when he seen blood on his hands.

"Bitch ass nigga!" The big man screamed, charging like a wild bull.

Mike took a few steps back before John was upon him. They grappled like wrestlers. Just when it looked like the bigger man had the advantage, Mike ducked down and thrust his head into John's gut. John's eyes bulged as the wind was forced from his lungs. Before he had a chance to recover, Mike lifted his head. Bone crunched when John's face met the back of Mike's head. Teeth flew and John's face opened up like a smashed watermelon. He was out before he hit the ground.

"Oh shit!" Vito yelled.

"Yeah, bitch ass nigga!" Junior screamed, jumping up and down excitedly.

"Pussy ass nigga!" Mike said, kicking John in the head.

I grabbed Mike and wrestled him to my car. It was time to go!

***

"I think I need to go to the hospital, brah," Mike said, grimacing as he touched the back of his head.

I took my eyes off the road to glance at him. "What's up? You good?"

"Nah. I think one of that nigga teeth stuck in the back of my head."

I clicked on the interior light. "Let me see. "

54

Mike turned his head and Sure enough, there was a small piece of a tooth object in the back of his head. "Yeah, man. That's a tooth."

Panic shown in his eyes. "Damn, Rob. Take me to the hospital. What if that nigga got AIDS or some shit! Know the mouth is the nastiest part of our body."

"A'ight. Soon as we get to Milwaukee."

"Hell nah! Fuck that shit, brah. Take me to the hospital right now. I need to get this shit out my head. What if that nigga got gum disease or something?"

"A'ight. Look on yo' phone for—"

Flashing lights in my rear-view mirror made me swallow my words. There was a police car burning up the highway about a quarter mile away. "You still got Junior gun?"

"Yeah, why?" Mike asked, lowering his head to look at the side mirror. When he seen the police car, he panicked. "Shit! You think they finna sweat us?"

"I don't know, but we about to find out in a few seconds."

"Driver, pull the car over!" The officer directed over the loudspeaker.

I slowed down and began pulling to the side of the highway.

"Damn, Rob! Fuckin with this nigga Junior," Mike panicked. "I should break on his ass."

I looked around to see if he had a chance at getting away. The highway was surrounded by woods. And not only that, but several more police cars were also speeding in our direction. "I don't know about this one, brah. He got back up and these woods don't look nigga friendly."

Mike slapped the seat in frustration. "Damn. I can't believe I'm 'bout to catch a case for this nigga. You should hide the pistol in yo' car."

"I can't, brah. I'm a felon. If I get caught with that gun, I'm going back to prison. And now that they got those federal gun laws for felons, I could get slammed."

"Driver, cut the engine and drop the keys out of the window!" The officer called over the bullhorn.

I looked through the side mirror as I dropped the keys out the window. The cop was standing behind the driver's door, aiming a gun at my car. The other officers pulled up and also pulled guns.

"Damn, Rob. They finna shoot us, my nigga," Mike stressed.

I was too scared to respond but I was thinking the exact same thing. We were on the highway alone at midnight. They could gun us down and probably get away with it.

"Driver, get out of the car and lie on the ground!"

I wish I would have stayed in Sapphire's bed.

Chapter 8

Heaven

My hands trembled as I fumbled with the envelope. I got nervous every time one of them showed up in my mailbox. And every time I opened one of them, I was overcome by the same two feelings. Optimism and Pessimism. When I was finally able to get the envelope open, I went directly to the final page to read the results. According to the DNA test, Ron was not the father of Jason. The second set of papers read the same thing for Mason. "Dammit!" I cursed, throwing the papers on the kitchen table.

Reading negative test results always made me feel like trash. After testing sixteen men and getting sixteen letters, I'm surprised that I wasn't immune to receiving bad news. But I wasn't. And every time I got a negative result, it felt like I died a little more inside. I couldn't believe I was out there so bad that. How many men I would have to test? Then the doubt crept in, and I started wondering if I was ever going to find him. I even considered giving up the search. The process was so emotionally draining.

"Please help me get through this, Lord," I prayed. "Please let me find my boy's father. I don't want my kids to die. Give me a sign or show me the way, Father."

After saying the prayer, I sat at the kitchen table and began staring at a spot on the wall that I'd never noticed before. I tortured myself with thoughts of my past life until I couldn't take it anymore.

"Get it together, Heaven," I told myself, getting up from the table.

I grabbed the papers and threw them in the garbage before heading to the living room. I needed to do something to take my mind off the bad DNA news. Ray and the twins were by a church members house attending a sleep over party and I was home alone. I thought about going out, but I didn't have anywhere to go. My kids, Ray, and my job had become my life. There was no such thing as free time when raising twins and a teenager. I had become a home body and now that I had some free time, I didn't know what to do with myself. After weighing my options, I was torn between writing a poem or responding to Lay-Lay's letter. Ever since I could remember, I loved poetry. When I started running the streets, I stopped writing and neglected my true love. After I changed my life, poetry became my outlet and I fell in love with it all over again.

I also liked writing to Lay-Lay. We had exchanged a few letters and I found myself looking forward to reading his thoughts and responding back. He was a good writer and knew how to express himself eloquently. Sometimes I didn't want the letters to end. His words were gentle, his thoughts were passionate, and he was very intelligent. I adored those qualities about him. I wasn't used to seeing that side of men. And the more I got to know him, the more I found myself wishing that he was the twin's father. That would make my life so much easier. But we were still waiting on test results. Until then, all I could do was wait and hope. Thinking of Lay-Lay made my decision easier. I put on my Trey Songz playlist and grabbed my laptop. Before I knew it, I was telling him about me and Ray's latest beef over the D-minus he got in math. Now his coaches were talking about not letting him play football if he didn't get his grades up. I had just finished telling the story when my phone rang. It was my best friend, Reesy.

"Hey, love," I answered.

"Hey, you," she sang.

I could hear the smile through the phone. Talking to her always put me in a good mood. She was a happy person and her happiness was infectious.

"What cha up to?" She asked.

58

"Writing Laron. My man and the kids are at a slumber party, so I got the house to myself." Reesy laughed at me calling Ray my man. "Well, that's good that you get a much-needed break from them. You have to have time to yourself."

"I thought the same thing, until they left. Now I don't have anything to do. They are my life." "Well, how about we start working on getting you a new life? And we can start tonight."

I wasn't sure what she meant. "What?"

"You need to get out of the house. Sister Johnson told me about the slumber party last Sunday. I was the one that told her to approach you about letting the boys go. You need some time to yourself. What do you say about coming out on the town with me tonight? I'm in the mood for some mental stimulation."

In my past life that meant a lot of things. "Mental stimulation?"

"Oh, did I say something wrong?"

"No. I just want you to clarify,"

"I know an open mic place downtown. People come in and do jazz, poetry, or sing. It'll be fun."

"Don't know. You know I'm not the going out type anymore."

"Oh, come on, woman! Live a little. I promise, it'll be fun. Just give it a chance. Plus, you need to get out of the house. Enjoy life while you're still young."

She did have a point. I really needed to get out of the house. I hadn't been out in so long that I forgot what going out felt like. I never did anything for myself anymore. I was scared to let loose. Scared that if I had too much fun, I might slip back into my old ways. Like I had done when I slept with Robert. That's why I always played it safe. But now that Reesy was asking, I kind of wanted to go out with her and explore the night. At least this time I knew my wing woman wouldn't let me do anything harmful.

"Okay, Reesy. You win. I'll go."

"Hooray!" She celebrated. "The place is called Tanna's. It's downtown. Real nice place. No thugs or hoochie mamas. Just good clean people looking to have good clean fun."

"What time do you want me to meet you there?" I asked, going over in my head what I was going to wear. I didn't have a big wardrobe. Mostly jeans and t-shirts.

"Girl, you are not going to believe this?" Reesy cackled like a witch.

I wanted to know what was so funny. "Why are you laughing?"

"It just so happens that I'm on the highway heading to your house. I'll be there in about ten minutes."

"You set me up."

"No, baby. It wasn't a setup. This is a jail break. I'm setting you free," she laughed again.

I school my head. "Okay. I'm going to get dressed. I'll see you when you get here."

After saying our goodbyes, I hung up and dashed to the shower to freshen up. Before I could finish getting Zest fully clean, I heard the front door open. Reesy had a spare key.

"I'm here, Heaven," she called.

"I'll be out in a minute."

"Take your time, love. I want us to get there around ten o'clock."

After the shower I put some Design Essentials conditioner in my hair to lock in my natural curls before going to find something to wear. Settled on a purple Donna Karen pant suit, a white blouse, and white Dior peep-toe heels. When I was satisfied with my clothes, I went to the mirror to put on my lashes, a little blush, and bubble gum flavored lips gloss.

"My goodness! You are a beautiful woman," Reesy complimented when I walked in the living room.

"Am I over doing it?" I asked, ready to change into a pair of jeans and a T-shirt.

"Oh no. Goodness, no. The pant suit is perfect. Make me go home and change."

I took the compliment to the heart because Reesy was very beautiful. She had honey colored skin, a small round face, and thick eyebrows that I would kill for. She was forty-five years old but could easily pass for a woman in her thirties. And not only was she beautiful, but she also had style. She wore dark jeans, a white T-shirt with 'Got Jesus' stenciled across the front, and black heels. But it wasn't what she was wearing, it was how she wore it. She had class and made everything look high fashion. There was a grace about this woman that exuded in her every movement. She was also smart, funny, and had been married to the love of her life for fifteen years. And like me, she also had a past.

"Alright. Let me grab my keys and purse and we can get out of here."

"So, did you ever get those test results back for that Ron guy?" Reesy asked as we stepped outside.

I turned to lock the front door. "I got them back today. He is not the father."

Reesy looked pained. "I'm sorry to hear that, love. Did you have your hopes up for this one?"

"No, not really. I don't get my hopes up anymore. I can't. I don't want to feel the letdown I felt the first couple of times."

Reesy hit the alarm on her charcoal gray Infiniti truck as we walked over. "What about the guy in prison? His results come back yet?"

"No. Probably another week or two," I said as we climbed in the truck.

"What do you think? Is there a chance?"

"I don't know. They don't look like him, but I guess anything is possible."

she reached over to grab my hand. "Don't give up, baby. Whatever you do, don't give up hope. Jason and Mason need you to keep looking. You hear me?"

I locked eyes with her and seen the love and care she had for me and my family. "I won't lose hope. I can't. They're going to get that operation and beat the disease. God is all powerful and all amazing."

"Amen!" Reesy agreed, giving my hand a squeeze before pressing the start button. "Keep that faith, love! Keep that faith! God will make a way. You know, my life ain't been no crystal stair. I did all the drugs, I was a prostitute and stripper, I had three abortions, been to jail, and I still don't know who my oldest child's father is. But you know what the beautiful thing about God is? When you come to him, he will take all of your mess and turn it into a message. Just look at what God did with me. I married the love of my life and went back to school and got a bachelor's degree. When people see me, they think I grew up living the perfect little princess life. Only if they knew. But God made a way for me, and he'll do the same for you."

I loved hearing Reesy talk about everything that she went through and how she came out on the other side. "Awe, thanks, Reesy," I gushed. "You are my inspiration."

"Glad to hear it," she said, pulling away from my house. "And now that you're feeling better, how about you finally bless the world with your gift of spoken word?"

I gave her 'the look'. "I knew this was some kind of set up. You think you're slick."

"It's not a setup, love. You need to be heard. You have a gift. Let it make room for you. Your poetry is good, and I think you should share it."

"But I'm not ready. And I don't want to share it."

"Why not?"

"Because it's personal. It tells my story. A story that I don't want everybody to hear."

"But it could be a blessing to somebody. And you don't have to tell one of your deep ones. Just give them enough. You can speak to people's souls and spirits. Like the one about you thinking about being lonely in a room full of people. What was it called?"

"Just thinking."

"Yeah. That one. Every woman on earth would love that."

I got flutters in my gut. "I don't know, Reesy."

"Trust me, Heaven. I love you. You are my sister, and I wouldn't ever give you bad advice. Show the world your gift. You are a blessing."

I caved. "Okay. I'll do it."

"Yes, love!" Reesy celebrated. "What you have is a gift from God, Heaven. We are supposed to use what we have to bless and help people. Otherwise, what's the point in having the gift?"

I was going back and forth in my head about whether or not I would 'show the world my gift'. I was more nervous than I had ever been in my life, and we hadn't even pulled up to the open mic place. "I know. But I'm still nervous."

Reesy grabbed my hand. "Tonight is about fun, sweety. Just relax and when you get upon that stage, let go and let God. You have a wellspring of strength that God placed inside of you that you haven't even tapped into yet. Trust God, baby. He will see you through."

That's why I loved Reesy. She always knew what to say.

When we walked into Tanna's, I immediately fell in love with the lounge. It was a small place that felt intimate. The lights were dim, and candles were glowing atop small tables spaced around the room. A band was on the stage playing soft jazz music. On the left wall was a bar. The people were dressed elegantly. The men in suits or casual looks. The women wore pantsuits, skirts, and nice gowns. The atmosphere was relaxed. And in spite of the good vibes I was feeling, I was still looking around nervously, waiting for someone from my past to pop out and ruin the evening before it started.

"So, what do you think? It's not too much for you, is it?" Reesy asked.

"No. I like it. We won't have to worry about nobody getting shot tonight," I cracked.

After our laugh, we went to the bar where I signed up to recite a poem and we order nonalcoholic fruit drinks. When we had our cocktails, we found an empty table in the front row and sat down.

"Good evening, ladies and gentlemen. My name is DJ Ricky-Rick and I'm your host for the night. For those that don't know, tonight is open mic night. Come on up here and do what you do. All we ask is that you keep it clean. We—"

My attention was grabbed away from the emcee when I thought I recognized a familiar face in the crowd. But before I could get a good look at him, he vanished. I tried to be inconspicuous as I searched the crowd for him. I was about to give up trying to find him when I felt someone watching me. I turned to my right and there he was. About twenty feet away. My night had just been ruined.

Chapter 9

Robert

"What up, Rob?" Junior greeted, smiling as we embraced.

"Chillin'. What's up with you, brah? I see you clean up nice," I said, wiping a piece of lint off his blue suit jacket.

He struck a few poses. "When you step out in Armani, that drip create rivers, boy!"

I popped the collar on my Gucci sweater. "C'mon, man. You don't know nothing about no drip."

"Let's get in here so you can watch me do my thang," Junior said before leading the way into the lounge.

I took a look around as I followed him inside. It had a coffee shop feel to it. Candles on the tables and a live band playing soft music. The name of the place was Tanna's. It was an open mic spot that Junior came to share poetry. I had never heard of the place, but he invited me to watch him perform. Since I didn't have anything to do, I agreed.

"I can get used to this," I said, nodding my head along to the music.

Junior smiled and waved at a few women that walked by. "This is an exclusive spot, Rob. Can't bring Mike and Vito to a place like this. They wouldn't appreciate it. I'm like a celebrity in here. Whatever you need, I can make it happen."

"How about you make a drink fall into my hands."

He nodded towards the bar. "Follow me."

The bartender was a tall brown skinned woman with a short natural afro and big brown eyes. "Hey, Junior! How you doing, sweety?" She smiled.

Junior turned extra cool, leaning against the bar and flashing the smile that he thought would make his modeling career. "Chillin'. 'Sup with you, Monica? You killing 'em with that natural, baby."

"Awe, thanks, baby." She blushed. "So, what can I get you?"

"Gimmie a glass of that Chardonnay."

She looked to me. "You want anything?"

"I'll take a Miller High Life."

"Okay, fellas. Be right back."

When the bartender left, Junior turned to me. "So, when are you going to bless the world with your gift, brotha?"

I chuckled, wondering what he was talking about. "What you on, man?"

"I'm talking about that voice, brah. I heard you talking to moms about it. She said you can sing. Why you never let yo' boys know?"

I adjusted nervously. "What is you talking about?"

He gave an irritated look. "C'mon, brah. I just told you. I know you got some pipes. Why you keeping it a secret?"

"When you supposed to have heard this conversation?"

"A while ago. But that's not important. Why you never told nobody you could sing?"

I decided to keep it real with my boy. "You know how it is growing up in the hood. They think singers is soft, so I kept it to myself."

"Man, we knew each other all this time and I can't believe you hid yo' gift from us. We struggled together, for real. Me, you, and Vito did hard time in Racine Correctional Institution. Shared secrets. Shed tears. Had each other's backs. We yo' boys, man. We would'da never looked at you differently because you could sing."

"I never thought about it like that. I always kept off to myself."

"You told us about Roger, and I know that was hard for you. We would'da supported you gettin' yo' Jacquees on, man. That's a gift, brah. And that's why I brought you out with me tonight. Mike and Vito can't appreciate talent like ours."

"I hear you. And I appreciate the love. I guess I was ashamed. And I got stage fright, for real. I know if I would'da told y'all, y'all would'da put me on the spot and I wasn't ready for that."

He nodded. "Yeah, we might've. But that's what friends do. So, when you gon' let me hear you? Tonight is as good a night as any."

I was about to answer when the bartender came with our drinks.

"Are you performing tonight?" Monica asked, smiling at Junior like she wanted to eat him.

"Yeah. I have a piece that I just finished. But I'm trying to get my boy to show the world what he can do," he said, turning the attention to me.

I wanted to splash him with my beer. He had done exactly what I didn't want him to do. "Ooh, you do spoken word?" Monica asked, excitement lighting her eyes.

"Nah, I'm not the word smith," I mumbled, trying to get the attention off me.

Junior refused to let me off the hook. "He sing."

I mugged him.

"Ooh, I love singers! Will you let me hear you?" Monica asked, her eyes wide with expectation.

"Uh, how about we play it by ear."

She looked disappointed. "I hope you do. Sometimes we have talent execs in here looking for new acts. You could be the next big thing."

"Yeah. Maybe," I said dryly, taking a sip of the beer.

"I have to get back to work. Let me know if you need anything else," she said before moving down the bar.

I gave Junior a little shove. "I just told you I didn't want to be put on the spot, fool."

He laughed. "C'mon, man. I'm just trying to help you get out of that shell. I used to have stage fright, too. The only way to get over it is to just get up there and do it."

I did need to get over my stage fright. My mother had been telling me that for years. It was holding me back. Not using my gift was kind of like abusing it. And it was contradicting for me to tell kids to chase dreams and overcome fears, yet I still hadn't conquered mine. "What the hell, man. Where do I sign up at?"

"Yeah, boy! That's what I'm talking about!" He celebrated. "Monica, come back over here and put my boy name on that chalk board!"

After signing up to participate in the show, we went to find seats.

"So, how everything going on your end, Rob? The fam good?"

I thought about my father and my mood became a little cloudy. "Yeah, I guess. Me and pop been talking."

"That sounds like a good thing, brah. You ain't talked to him in a minute. Why you don't sound happy about it?"

"'Cause he dying."

Junior looked at me like I just told him I helped crucify Jesus. "What? You serious?"

"Yeah, man," I nodded. "Terminal cancer. They said he got about a year."

"Damn, Rob. I don't know what to say."

"Me either. Ain't nothing you can really say. Let's switch lanes. How you doing? Everything cool with you, Amber, and Marrissa?"

He lowered his head for a moment. When he looked up again, I could see emotion in his eyes. "Man, I gotta thank y'all for coming through for me. I had that Henny in me and I almost messed up."

"Wasn't nothing, brah. We yo' boys. Couldn't let you go back to the joint. Besides you would'da did the same thing for us. We just gotta hope they don't be too hard on Mike."

Junior's face lit up. "Man, I didn't know our boy could throw hands like that. Family is the truth!"

"I never seen him lose a fight. I just wish yo' baby mama neighbors wasn't snitches. Highway patrol pulled so many guns on us that I thought they was the SWAT Team."

"That was the good side of Madison. Know they coming with them guns out for anything involving black people. I feel bad about him catching a case trying to save my ass."

"I think he'll be good. He never been in trouble before. This his first case. They probably give him some probation or something."

"Man, I hope so. I hate to see my dog go down for me. I ain't that kind of nigga. I take my own weight."

"Don't trip, brah. Mike already said he good. He know they not gon' slam a first time felon. Amber need you out here, not doing five to ten. We all gon' to get through this."

"Yeah, you right," he breathed heavily. "I don't know what Amber would've done without me."

We got lost in thought and I let my eyes roam over the crowd. That's when I saw her.

"Good evening, ladies and gentlemen. My name is DJ Ricky-Rick and I'm your host for the night. For those that don't know, tonight is—"

I tuned the emcee out as I watched Heaven, visions of our last encounter playing in my head. She looked even better than I remembered. She must've felt me watching her because she began looking around. Like she was searching for me. And then she found me. Her gray eyes held my attention. I felt a connection with her. Then she looked away.

"Ay, ain't that shorty you left the bar with a lil' while ago?" Junior asked.

I couldn't hide the smile. "Yeah. That's Heaven."

"Rob, shorty is bad! Damn! You say you didn't hit that, huh?" He asked, cocking a brow and giving me a suspicious look.

"C'mon, man." I shook my head. "I told y'all I blacked out. I don't know what happened."

"Okay, okay. I know you was—"

I watched Junior's lips moving but I had tuned him out. I was too busy going over what I was going to say to Heaven. Something happened when we locked eyes. Like something inside of me connected with something inside of her.

"You know what I'm sayin'?" Junior laughed, slapping me on the shoulder.

"You a fool, brah!" I laughed, acting like I knew what he was talking about.

Our laughter calmed when the emcee began calling acts upon the stage. The first performance was a political rap by a young Asian. His sound was influenced by Killer Mike and he got a nice ovation. Next was a tall skinny white guy with dreadlocks. He sang an old Bob Marley song. A few performers later, it was Junior's turn.

"Wish me luck, brah!" He said, taking one last sip from his drink before walking away. He swaggered to the stage with the confidence of a superstar. After giving the crowd a smile, he began began to speak. "Good evening, ladies and gentlemen. I'm going to recite a poem called 'making music'.

If life exists in your voice, then you must continue to sing to me.

Sustain my organs with your sweet melodies and paint pictures of your dreams for me.

Sing a song for my heart to fill it with joy, A tune for my ears to remove the bleak. Transfer emotions trim your depths to mine with a melody that makes me move my feet.

Awaken my deepest senses with your octaves without instruments.

Her lips more beautiful than pleasure and skin looks kisses by cinnamon.

She kissed me, and like a flute her breath passed through me and made music.

I banged her bongos all night long until her songs became lucid.

She danced on my trombone!

She danced on my trombone like she had high notes deep inside her.

And every time I thrust, her high notes got like Mariah's. Even higher!

Crescendo than climax as I played or orgasmic organ.

Fingering her keys of pleasure like a greater pianist. Making music."

The crowd gave him a standing ovation. Junior took a bow before swaggering from the stage. I loved my boy's wordplay. He was by far the best poet I'd ever heard.

"That was hot, brah!" I yelled over the applause, giving him a hug.

"Thanks, man. I penned that a couple days ago. I wasn't sure if I was going to be able to pull it off, but they loved it."

"You the truth, brah!"

We had seats as the emcee started speaking again. "Junior, you did your thing, boy! Okay, y'all. Let's get ready for the next act. Coming to the stage next is Heaven." My eyes flew in her direction. She looked caught off guard when he said her name. She stood slowly, keeping her eyes on he floor as she walked upon the stage. When she grabbed the mic, I noticed a nervous twitch on the right side of her mouth. Then she cleared her throat.

"This is a poem I wrote a few years ago called Just Thinking.

I was just thinking... About everything and nothing as my mind ran wild like a child on a sugar high.

I thought about how fast we moved into a blissful union and how quickly it ended with the pain of heart ache.

You see, he gave me his rhythm of life prematurely and I dived in headfirst.

It didn't matter that I was here, and he was there.

The only thing that mattered was being together.

We never thought past our greeting kiss and always thought about each other after we kissed goodbye.

Our love was art.

A priceless masterpiece painted by the fingers of the Master himself.

Just thinking about him makes my life a reoccurring ending to Daylight Savings: My days are shorter and nights are longer.

I was just thinking... If time, either too much or not enough, changes the outcome of our dreams, than why do we dream?

Has our time apart changed the way you dream of me?

I was just thinking...How insane it sounds to be lonely in a room full of people and how, without you, I feel lonely and insane.

I've heard that loneliness isn't the absence of affection but the absence of direction.

If that's true, than I'm lost...

Because you were my compass."

When Heaven finished the poem, the crowd went wild like they just heard Whitney Houston come out the grave and do a final performance. The women whistled and screamed like she had created a new mantra. And the look on Heaven's wide eyes and dropped jaw showed how surprised she was by the crowd's reaction.

"She raw, brah." Junior smiled.

I nodded in agreement as she left the stage. I wanted her in the worst way.

Chapter 10

Heaven

It felt like I had been strapped to a rocket and sent into outer space!

I had done a lot of drugs in my life, but none of them compared to the high I got from being on that stage. Performing my poetry in front of people gave me a rush I had never felt before. I felt really-really good. And seeing the people stand and clap for me made me feel like a star.

"You did great! How do you feel?" Reesy asked, wrapping me in a bear hug.

I said the only word that came to mind. "Amazing."

She hugged me again. "Ain't you glad that I broke you out of jail?"

"Sometimes you know what you're talking about."

She gave me a proud look before we sat back down.

"Alright, y'all. We gotta keep the good vibes flowing," the emcee said. "Coming to the stage is another newcomer at Tanna's. This is Junior's best friend so let's show some love for Robert!"

My eyes found him quickly. I didn't know he was performing, but I was very interested to see what kind of talent he had. He walked towards the stage with a confident swagger. A confidence that I didn't see the morning after our deed. He was well groomed and wore a nicely fitted red, green, and gold Gucci sweater with dark slacks and loafers.

"Y'all expect me to follow that?" He asked, looking at me and bringing a laugh from the crowd. "I'ma try to do some justice by singing a timeless classic. This is Must Be Nice by Lyfe Jennings."

After clearing his throat, Robert closed his eyes and blew my socks off when he opened his mouth. His voice had a perfect tenor tone. Smooth and strong. He showed range and control as he sang a beautiful acapella version of the song. God had truly blessed him with a gift. I was in awe and couldn't take my eyes off of him. When he finished, I stood with the rest of the crowd and applauded my approval. He looked humbled by our reaction as he waved and walked from the stage. I decided to throw caution to the wind. I watched Robert until we locked eyes. There was something between us that I wanted to explore. When the next performer walked upon the stage, I took my cue.

"I need to get another drink, Reesy. Want me to get you something?"

"No. I'm good. I'm enjoying the show," she said, wiping tears from her eyes.

"You okay?"

"Yeah. That song was beautiful and it touched my spirit."

I walked in Robert's direction. We made eye contact again. I smiled and turned for the bar. Out of my peripheral, I could see him get up from his table. Bees, hornets, and butterflies began buzzing around in my stomach as I anticipated our encounter.

"Mph! Girl, you tore down the house!" The bartender laughed, raising her hand for a high five.

"Thank you," I said as we slapped hands. "Can I have another cranberry juice with a lemon twist?"

"You can have anything you want," a familiar voice said from behind me.

I turned and seen Robert walking towards me. He wore a bright smile and our eyes stayed locked like we had magnets in them. "Can I get a Miller with that cranberry juice?" He asked the bartender. "Heaven, that poem was... The best I ever heard. And don't tell my boy, but you're my favorite poet."

We shared a laugh. "Thank you, Robert. You know, I haven't heard that song in years. And you sang it better than Lyfe."

His face turned a shade darker. "Thank you. You know, I thought about not even going up there? I Never sang in front of nobody except a hand full of people. That was my friend's first time hearing me sing and I've known him for about ten years."

"Wow. It sounds like you could sing professionally. You have a gift. And do you want to hear something crazy?"

He looked at me expectantly. "I do."

"That was my first time performing in front of people, too. I was so nervous that I almost threw up."

He laughed. "I felt the exact same thing. I was praying that my voice didn't crack. I would've hated to get booed off stage during my first performance. That would've been a nightmare."

We shared another laugh. Then the bartender showed up with our drinks. "Here is your cranberry. And here is your Miller. By the way, that was a great performance, Robert. You have a really nice voice."

"Thank you." He nodded, sitting a twenty-dollar bill on the bar.

"Be right back with your change."

When the bar tender left, an uncomfortable silence came and stood in between us. It felt like we both had something to say but we were waiting for the other one to speak first. I needed him to know that I wasn't a thot so I took the lead.

"Look, Robert. I don't know what you think of me, but I don't normally do what we did."

"You wanna hear something crazy?" He chuckled.

My heart began beating faster and harder. "What?"

"I don't normally do what we did either. Before that night, I had been celibate for fourteen months."

My eyes grew wide with surprise. I had never met a celibate man before. And the bigger shock was two celibate people unknowingly sleeping together. Now I understood why he was so nervous the morning after. "I'm not trying to make this moment any crazier than it already is, but I was also celibate before that night. For five years."

His eyes grew wider than mine. "What are the chances?"

"I know, right? I'm freaking out a little bit, too. So, what were you doing in that bar the night we met?"

"My boys talked me into it. I stopped clubbing about a year ago. After I got serious with God. Don't get me wrong, I love kicking it with my boys, but I got tired of the same thing. I was tired of being a rebel without a cause. The cheap thrills stopped being exciting. I was yearning for something deeper. I wanted to find somebody that wanted me for me. Not because I looked a certain way or because of what I had."

I was blown away by his words. This man was preaching to the choir. "I'm surprised to hear a man saying that. I've run into so many men that only want to smash and run. To hear that is refreshing."

"Not all of us are like that, Heaven. Still some good guys out here. So, tell me about you. Why did you become celibate?"

There was no way I was telling him the truth. "How much time do you have? This will take all night," I joked, stalling to figure out how much I should say.

"I have as much time as you need."

"I guess my story is similar to yours. Got tired of the lies. Got tired of meeting men that only wanted one thing. Then, once I got pregnant with my boys, I knew it was time for something different. So, I focused on bettering myself and my relationship with God."

He smiled at my response. "I never thought that I would meet someone I had so much in common with. You go to church?"

"Every Sunday. You?"

"Yep. Mount Zion Baptist Church. Haven't missed a service in over a year."

I looked down at the bottle of beer in his hand. My pastor preached abstinence from alcohol.

"Don't be looking at my drink like that. Quote me one scripture that says, 'Thou shall not drink beer'."

I laughed at the joke. I liked him and enjoyed his company way more than I expected. "So, what do you do for a living, Robert. I remember you having a nice whip on chrome."

"I'm a welder. Been doing that for a couple years. And I do a little motivational speaking on the side."

"Wow. That's so cool. What made you get into motivational speaking?"

"Life." He chuckled. "I've been through some things. My teenage years tested my mom and pop. I made a lot of mistakes and I want to use what I learned to stop other kids from making the mistakes I did."

He seemed too good to be true. "Are you for real?"

He laughed. "Are you? Everything you thinking about me, I'm thinking about you."

"How old are you?"

"I'm twenty-nine. You?"

"I'm twenty-six. You mentioned your parents. Are they still together?"

"Yeah. They been together for thirty-two years. They set the example of what love is supposed to be like. And I don't know how my mother put up with my dad for so long. She's a very patient woman."

"There you are," Reesy said, popping up at my side. "I was wondering what happened to you."

"Oh, I'm sorry, Reesy," I apologized.

"It's okay, love." She smiled, looking to Robert. "Twenty years ago, if he would've started talking to me, I would've probably ditched you, too."

"Reesy, this is Robert. Robert, this is my best friend and angel, Reesy," I introduced.

"Nice to meet you." He smiled, extending a hand.

"Like wise. You have a very beautiful voice, young man. The only time I cry is at church, but you made me shed a few tonight. Good job."

"I'm sorry to have made you cry but I'm also honored."

Reesy turned to me. "He's a good one. I'm going to finish catching the show. Find me when you're done."

"Okay. I'll be over soon." When Reesy walked away, I turned to Robert. "Listen, um... I have to get back to my girl. Can I... I was wondering if..."

"Can I see your phone?" He asked, seeing my struggle.

I pulled my phone from my pocket.

"Unlock it and I'll type my number into for you."

I unlocked it and handed him the phone. He began dialing and then his phone rang.

"Can you accept calls at any time? No curfews, right?"

"Ha-ha, funny. I don't have curfews. I'm a grown woman."

"Okay then, grown woman. I'll call you."

"Do that. Talk to you later."

I walked away feeling like I had finally met MRightght. Robert was handsome, educated, funny, spiritual, and very respectful. We had so much in common that it felt uncanny. When I got back to the table, Reesy was smiling.

"Seems like a nice young man."

"Yeah. He's cool," I said, trying to act nonchalant.

"Look at you trying to play cool." Reesy laughed. "You're doing a bad job, love. You are blushing and glowing like you fell in love."

"Stop playing." I laughed. "It's not even like that."

"Ha! Tell me anything. You over there grinning like you won the Powerball! Tell me about him. What does he do? Where is he from? Does he go to church?"

I couldn't wait to blab about him. "He's twenty-nine, works as a welder and motivational speaker. He also goes to Mount Zion Baptist Church and hasn't missed a service in a year. Oh, and his parents have been together for thirty-two years. And he's celibate."

Reesy looked surprised. "Wow, Heaven. He sounds like the perfect man. Now aren't you glad that I got you up out of that house?"

"Yeah, yeah, yeah. I owe you a big thanks for helping me get out of my own way. Thank you."

She nodded. "You know, Heaven, sometimes God has a funny way of showing up right in the middle of our ordinary lives and doing some extraordinary things."

I couldn't have said it any better.

Chapter 11

Robert

"I know some of y'all looking at me and saying, 'He don't know how it is in the hood.' Or, 'He don't know what it's like to struggle or lose somebody he love to the streets.' Or, 'He don't know what it's like to do time.' And I want all of y'all that had those thoughts to know that y'all wrong."

I paused to look out over the hundreds of teenage faces that packed the auditorium. I was doing a speaking gig at Custer High School. I had been speaking for almost fifteen minutes and for the most part, I managed to keep their attention.

"The worst thing you can do is judge a book by its cover. Nah, I don't talk slick or wear a bunch of drip, but make no mistake, I got the hood running through my veins. I jumped off the porch when I was fourteen. Started hustling when I was sixteen. Mom and pop didn't want to buy me J's so I went out and got it myself. When I seen how fast that money came, I quit school. Started kicking it on 41st and Center and tried to run it up. Full time grind. Everything was going my way. I was looking good and riding good. Then them L's came. Hit me hard. Worst pain I ever felt in my life." I paused to clear my throat and fight off the tears that threatened to spill. "The streets took my brother."

When I looked over the crowd, I saw sympathetic faces staring up at me.

"Right after that, the police came for me. Ended up doing a five-year bid. Girl broke bad. The bros didn't come through. Matter of fact, some of my day ones was smashing my girl while I was down bad. Same ones I grew up and threw up with stabbed me in the back. I know what I'm talking about, y'all. Whatever y'all think l I don't understand, y'all wrong. I been there and done that. And I'm here to let y'all know it's a better way. You don't have to you through the hard knocks. You have a choice. I lost five years of my life doing it the wrong way. Five years that I won't ever get back. Ain't nothing cool about getting locked up and having to use the bathroom in front of a bunch of dudes. Ain't nothing cool about showering with twenty other dudes standing around a pole spraying water. Ain't nothing cool about getting stripped searched and having another man looking all in your butt because they feel like it. It's a better way. And it starts right here. With an education. I own a two hundred-thousand-dollar house. Want to know how? Because of an education. I got a pearl white, old school on twenty sixes. Wanna know why? An education. I got a welding job that pays me almost a seventy grand a year. I can buy everything the hustlers buy. And I don't gotta worry about the police or jackers taking it because I got insurance, and everything is paid for. If something happens to anything I own, I just come back harder. Listen to what I'm telling you. I did it the wrong way and now I'm doing it the right way. You got a choice."

When I started talking about the money, I grabbed their undivided attention. By the end of my speech, I knew that I had done my job. At least one of those kids would learn from my mistake. That was a win. After leaving the school, I drove to Walmart to pick up a few items I needed for the house. I was standing in the express lane, waiting to check out, when I saw her. She was three lanes over. Her back was towards me, but I knew it was her. I knew that curly hair, light skin, small waist, and big booty anywhere. I wanted to call to her, but I didn't want to seem thirsty. So, I waited in line, sneaking peaks, hoping we would make eye contact.

"Good afternoon, sir. Paper or plastic?" The young female cashier asked.

"Plastic is fine," I mumbled, sneaking another peak to lane four. She still hadn't turned toward me.

"That'll be 24.80."

I paid with a credit card.

"Thank you for shopping at Walmart. Have a nice day."

"You're welcome," I said quickly, grabbing my bags and heading for my dream girl. She was standing at the cash register going through her purse when I approached. I was about to call her name when she looked up. To my surprise and disappointment, it wasn't Heaven. We locked eyes for an awkward moment.

"Uh, do you have a family member named Heaven?" I asked, surprised by their resemblance.

She gave me the head to toe look that women sometimes gave men that were bothering them. "No. Do I know you?"

"Nah. My bad. I thought you were somebody else."

During the drive home, I couldn't stop thinking about Heaven. A couple days had passed since I seen her at Tanna's and for no other reason than being busy, I hadn't called her. But now that I had seen what could've been her sister, my desire for the real thing was intensified. So, I made the call.

"Hello?"

Damn, she sounded good. "Now I know why your mother named you Heaven. You truly do have the voice of an angel."

"Hey, Robert." She giggled. "How are you doing?"

"I'm good. How are you? Is everything okay?"

She let out a deep sigh. "No. My day isn't going so well. I've been dealing with some bad news."

Her words tugged at my heart. "What's going on? Do you need help?"

"I'm fine. It's work related. I'm just going to take an extended lunch."

I saw an opportunity. "Care for some company? I just finished speaking at a high school and I'm in a giving advice mood."

"Why not? I'm at Starbucks on East Capitol. I have about thirty minutes before I have to get back to work."

"I'll be there in ten."

***

I noticed her as soon as I walked through the doors. She was seated at a table not far from the counter. Even in the purple scrubs she stood out like a lioness in a pack of zebras.

"I didn't know they made designer scrubs," I joked, sliding into the chair across from her.

"Stop, Robert!" She blushed.

"Starbucks, huh? The world's most expensive coffee shop."

"I'm addicted to their Frappuccino," she said, holding up a cup. "So, where were you speaking?"

"Custer High School. My pastor knows the principal and hooked it up. I try to tell the kids about the pit falls of life in the streets. They don't really start listening until I start talking about my cars and how much money I make."

"That's how kids are today. Rap, movies, and videos are so materialistic. That's the culture. Your slacks and polo shirt don't scream 'I got money' so they don't respect you. They don't listen until you talk the language of the culture. Money. But let Lil' Baby or Moneybagg walk in there those kids would've been listening like God was talking."

"That's so messed up, ain't it? I wish you wasn't right, but you are. But as long as I reach one of them, I feel like I did my job. I wish I could save them all, but I know I can't. But enough about me. How are you doing? What's going on?"

The light in her gray eyes dimmed a little. "One of my patients died over night."

"I'm sorry to hear that. What happened?"

"Brain aneurysm. She was ninety-two."

"Wow. Ninety-two. I don't think you should be sad for her. She lived a full life and then some. Was she one of them hallelujahing, Jesus preaching, scripture quoting old ladies?"

"She was. And I know she's in heaven. I just miss her. She was more like a grandmother than a patient. I trusted her. She gave good advice and she always prayed with me and for me. God doesn't allow us to meet many people like that."

I felt her pain and heard it in her voice. "Yeah, I hear you. My mom is that person for me. But just so you know, you can trust me."

She looked like she wanted to say something but held her tongue.

"I know what it's like to lose someone close, Heaven. I lost too. And I haven't told many people this, but I'm about to lose my father. He has cancer."

Her face softened. "I'm sorry to hear that, Robert. How bad is it?"

"Stage four. They said he has about a year. Nothing nobody can do. It's messed up because we just patched up our relationship. We were estranged for eight years up until about a month ago."

She reached across the table and grabbed my hand. It was a small gesture, but it meant a lot.

"I'm sorry to hear that, Robert. That is so sad. I don't know what I would do if I was in your shoes."

"Nothing we can do but trust God."

"Amen," she agreed.

silence fell over us as I was consumed by thoughts of my father. I still had a hard time accepting that he was dying. It didn't feel real. I could feel my mood changing so I switched it up. "Enough about the dark stuff. How is your family? Ray and the twins?"

The light in Heaven's eyes returned at the mention of her family. "My little monsters are fine. I know all mothers say this, but my babies are angels. They don't give me any trouble. Everyone that comes in contact with them loves them. Ray, on the other hand, is a big ol' hand full. He's failing math so the coaches are talking about not letting him play football."

"That's messed up. You ever consider getting him a tutor? Sports and after school activities are important for a kid his age. Keeps them out of trouble and off the streets. An idle mind is the devil's playground."

"I know. I want him to stay on the team. I've seen him play and he's good. Plays defensive end and right guard. Coaches say he has a lot of potential, but at fifteen, he can't see past tomorrow. We argued about him failing math and I was about to get him a tutor, but he promised to do better. If his grades don't improve, I'm beating his butt."

I pictured Heaven trying to fight her little brother. The boy was a giant. In my vision, her attempt at beating him didn't go so well.

"What are you smiling at?"

"I was picturing you whooping Ray. Didn't go so good. Little dude is huge."

She mugged me. "I'm tougher than I look. Don't let my size and looks fool you. I can hang with the big boys."

She was trying to look serious but it made me laugh.

"Keep laughing, Robert. Keep thinking I'm sweet."

Her little bit of attitude was cute. I wanted more time with her. "When can I take you out?"

She looked caught off guard. "What?"

"When can I take you out?"

She became flustered. "Um, I don't know. The kids and Ray and my job. I don't really have time to... Um...I can't."

Wasn't expecting that. "Ouch." I winced, grabbing my chest.

"It's not like that, Robert. I just don't do the dating thing."

I searched her face trying to figure her out. We had already had sex, she gave me her phone number and met me on her lunchbreak, but she was flaking on me about a date. It didn't make sense. "So, what are we doing? I don't understand."

She took a moment to gather her thoughts. "I don't know what we're doing. You're cool, Robert, but I don't know how this is supposed to go. I've never had a boyfriend. I've never been on a date. I'm not sure if I can..."

I waited for her to continue, but she didn't. She looked stressed and flustered. Nothing she was doing or saying made sense to me. One moment she was cool and calm, and the next she was unsure.

"I'm sorry, Robert. I know I'm all over the place. I'm not trying to be mean. I'm celibate and... I don't know. I'm sorry, but I have to go."

"Heaven, wait!"

"I'm sorry, Robert, but I have to get back to work."

She was gone before I could say another word.

Chapter 12

Robert

"Let me know when you about to cum, baby. I gotta surprise for you," Sapphire said before shoving my stick back in her mouth.

I couldn't talk so I moaned my acknowledgment. Sapphire gave the best oral sex that I ever had. If there was a competition with a grand prize, I would sponsor her against any woman in the United States. Scratch that. I would sponsor her against any woman in the world. Move over, Super Head. Sapphire was the truth! I watched as she worked her jaws on me. She moaned and slurped while using her hands to stroke my shaft and massage my balls. Watching her bring me to the ultimate pleasure was captivating. Her movements were seductive. And it wasn't long before I felt the volcano about to erupt.

"Mmmm! I'm about to bust!" I warned, grabbing a fist full of the bedsheets.

Sapphire took me from her mouth and gave me a furious hand job. She lowered her head and began licking, sucking, and tonguing my prostate, the small area between my anus and nut sack. Felt so good I cursed.

"Oooh shhhiiittt!"

Sperm shot out of my tool like a geyser. Flew so high that I thought some would stick to the ceiling. It was all over my pelvis and lower abs. Some even landed in Sapphire's weave but she acted like she didn't notice as she continued to pump her fist until I was drained. "Damn, baby! I see yo' body was missing mama," she purred, kneeling over me and licking semen droplets from my abs.

"Damn, girl!" was all I could manage.

This was the reason I couldn't stay away from her. When it came to sex, she knew exactly what to do and how to do it.

"I see you ready for more, huh?" She asked, continuing to stroke my hard pole as she bit one of my nipples. "Scoot to the edge of the bed. Let me take care of you, baby."

I slid to the edge of the bed, placing my feet on the floor. Her beautiful backside bounced and jiggled as she climbed out of bed and grabbed a condom from the drawer. She ripped it open and slid it on me. When my man was covered, she spun around and sat down reverse cowgirl.

"Ssss! Yeah, baby!" She moaned.

Sapphire's box was on fire! Her inside felt so good that I wished I could package it in jars and put it on the market. We would be millionaires by tomorrow. She was hot, tight, and wet; a feat that surprised me because while I had no proof, I knew I wasn't the only one hittin' it. After her walls adjusted to me being inside, Sapphire went to work. She began slow, rocking her hips back and forth, picking up the pace with every stroke. A few moments later she was bent over, grabbing her ankles while bouncing her cakes on my lap. I held on, enjoying the best ride of my life. When we both got our rocks off, she cuddled up next to me and kissed me on the cheek.

"Do you feel better now?"

"Hell yeah, baby. You tapped me out," I yawned, closing my eyes, ready to go to sleep. "You know I love you, right?" She asked.

"I know, baby girl," I mumbled, keeping my eyes closed.

I knew she was watching me. I could feel her breath on my cheek. And this was the part of our evenings that I hated. The pillow talk. I had no love for Sapphire. None at all. My feelings for her were long gone. Our thing was strictly sexual. But she always found a way to bring up something about relationships and love.

"You ain't gon' say it back?" She asked, her voice cracking with emotion.

I wanted to say "Nope!" but I didn't feel like arguing. "You know we got that butter love, baby."

Apparently satisfied, she wrapped an arm around me and lay her head on my chest. "Sometimes I think you love my sex more than you love me."

If she had seen the smile spreading across my face or knew how truthful her statement, she might've cut me.

***

"Robert! Robert! Robert!"

I awoke to Marcus and Marcel rocking me. These were the kids that Sapphire somehow felt I was responsible for. Marcus was nine and Marcel was almost three.

"What's up, man? Why y'all waking me up?"

"You said you was gonna watch the Avengers movie with us the next time you was here!" Marcus said, tugging at my arm.

"C'mon, Robert. Please!" Marcel begged, sounding like he was about to cry.

"Gimmie a minute. Let me get dressed," I mumbled.

They ran from the room giggling. Seeing the brothers made me think of my childhood with my brother. We woke up every Saturday morning to watch cartoons. After a yawn and stretch I threw on my boxers. When I walked in the living room, the movie was just starting and the boys were sitting on the couch with big bowls of Captain Crunch in their laps. I made myself a bowl and joined them. For the next two hours we watched the movie and wrestled.

Marcus and Marcel weren't my kids even though Sapphire tried to convince me they were. Before I went to prison, I actually believed that Marcus was my son and had even grown to love the boy. It was only after Sapphire burnt me that I became suspicious that she was cheating. When I confronted her about it, she lied. Swore up and down that she hadn't burnt me and tried to flip the script and say I burnt her. But I knew I hadn't. I made sure to be careful and wear a condom if I slept with another woman. I figured since she was lying about burning me, that she was lying about everything else. So, when Marcus was around six months old, I snuck off to get a DNA test. I got the results a week later. When I found out he wasn't my son, it felt like my heart had been ripped from my chest. I wanted to kill Sapphire. We argued and she cried, insisting the results were wrong. But we knew the truth.

Fast forward to me getting out of prison and I started sleeping with her again, but making sure I wore a condom. She got pregnant a few months later and tried to put the baby on me again. Said the condom must've broke. I told her she was a liar and to get a DNA test. When Marcel was born, we got tested and it came back that he wasn't mine. I still wasn't sure if Sapphire knew who the boys' fathers were. If she did, she never told me. And for that matter, I never heard the boys mention their fathers. All they knew was me. I did what I could for the boys because I was sexing their mom, and they were good kids. But I refused to accept responsibility for them.

By noon I was back at home showering. Today, me and my boys were meeting at the YMCA to shoot hoops. This was a weekend ritual. We were very competitive, and I always looked forward to taking my boys to flight school. After the shower, I got dressed in sports gear. The late great Kobe Bryant was my favorite player, so I had lots of Kobe and Lakers gear. Today I wore Kobe's white Lakers jersey with a pair of white Kobe shoes. Also threw a head band and wrist band in my pocket with black mamba emblem on it.

After throwing on Nike sweats, I pressed the start button on my key chain to get the Buick warm. Cold car seats were my kryptonite. Even though it was November and technically wasn't winter, there was already an inch of snow on the ground. During a Mid-West winter, electronic start on the car was a must. By the time I stepped outside, the car was nice and warm. I was meeting the fellas at 2:00 and had some time to kill so I went to check up on my parents. They lived in Brown deer, a suburb outside Milwaukee. It took about twenty minutes to get home. After using the key to let myself in, I found both of my parents in the living room. Pop was in his chair watching college football and mom was on the couch reading a book. I greeted them with hugs and kisses.

"I don't know why you watching the University of Illinois play, pop. Ain't no good teams in Illinois. Ain't the Badger game on?" I teased.

Pop loved his alma mater, even though they were terrible. "Betta watch ya mouth, boy! I still got my service pistol," he threatened. "They gotta good team. Just make too many mistakes."

"Right. And you know scientists just figured out how to make money grow on trees,".

Dad gave me 'the look'.

"Leave your father alone, Robert. You know he is crazy about our school's football team," mom cut in. "Let him enjoy his sports."

"This ain't no sport, mama. The score is 17 to 48. This is a bloodbath. You wanna see sports, come watch me at the YMCA."

"Boy, if I was yo' age, I'd show you out on that court," pop jumped in. "Y'all don't even play basketball today. Just wanna score points. No fundamentals. And y'all all soft. Can't even take a foul. Cry like babies when somebody lay the wood on you. In my day, no blood no foul."

"Yeah, and back in y'all day, they used to have to give y'all enemas to remove those lil' shorts after every game," I laughed.

Pop looked like he wanted to do me bodily harm and that made me laugh harder. Laughed so hard I began crying.

Even mom got in on the laughter. The remote came flying but I was able to dodge it.

"Keep talking, trash and I'ma get up out his chair," pop threatened. "That's all y'all do now-a-days is run ya mouth. All talk. And give me back my remote."

"So, what brings you by the house, son?" Mom asked.

"Nothing. Just wanted to see how you and pop doing," I said, tossing pop the remote and making sure to keep some distance between us. My old man was vengeful.

"Your mother tells me you met a woman. Hopefully your choice in women has improved significantly," pop said. Improved significantly was code for better than Sapphire.

"Much better, pop. Heaven is cool."

"Heaven, huh? Hell of a name, son. Does she look the part?"

I thought about to describe her beauty in a way that pop would feel me. "If I had to choose between her and Beyonce, I'm kicking Bey to the curb."

Pop reacted like I slapped him. He had a thing for Mrs. Carter. "Get outta here, man!"

I didn't say a word. Just stared at pop, holding his eye contact. He caught on.

"Wooo-weeee! When you bringing her around?"

"Watch it, Fred!" Mom warned, giving pop the evil eye. I laughed.

"Awe, Ann, you know God broke the mold after he made you, baby. I just wanted to see if the boy got my taste," pop said, giving me a wink.

After hanging out with my parents for a little while, I headed to the YMCA to get my hoop on. I listened to Tha Carter IV during the drive. This was a ritual. Lil' Wayne always got me geeked up.

"Dere he is!" Vito called when I walked through the gymnasium doors.

All my boys were present; Mike, Junior, and Vito. "'Sup, y'all?" I greeted, giving everyone daps and pounds.

"Look at this nigga." Mike smirked, watching me as I took off the Nike sweat suit.

The look and comment were because of my Kobe gear. Mike and Junior hated the NBA great because of their love for the Buck's and The Greek Freak. I loved my home team as well as Giannis, but Kobe was still my favorite player. The Black Mamba was a beast!

"Don't hate. Getcha game up and I'll buy you some Kobe gear," I bragged, laying my cell phones on the bench next to my sweats before putting on my head band and wrist band. "Well, I hope all that Kobe trash help you play better because we got next," Junior said.

"Man, why you ain't leave dem phones in the car? Know it's some thirsty ass niggas up in here." Vito said, eyeing my phones.

"One is for my money and the other my lifeline," I explained, walking over and stripping the ball from Junior

"I ain't never seen you have a business conversation on that gray phone," Mike said. "Matter of fact, every time it ring, you ignore it."

Vito and Junior laughed.

I ignored the comment and focused on the hoops. "Who our fifth man?"

"We gon' pick up one from whatever team lose," Junior said.

I began warming up on the side court while keeping an eye on the main court, sizing up the competition. They were mostly young guys. A few of them looked like they didn't have a clue what was going on. Then someone caught my eye. He was about 6'6" with good fundamentals. And his team was losing. And by the look of the winning team, we would need all the help we could get. Vito was thirty-four with bad knees. Wore braces on both of them. His best asset was his jumper. When he was on, nobody could stop him.

Junior was good on defense but offensively challenged. Mike had game and could play with the best of them. And I held my own. I didn't rock Kobe gear for nothing. Could've played division one had I gone to college. But instead of following hoop dreams, the streets took me under. When the game was over, my squad took the court along with the big youngster. We won four in a row. Would've won the fifth but I got tired. After our loss, we headed to the bench to rest up.

"Man, I feel like I'm thirty-four!" Vito breathed heavily.

I gave him a sideways look. "You are thirty-four, fool."

"I know. But I look good though." He laughed.

"Ay, Rob? What's this shit I hear about you singing like Chris Brown, nigga?" Mike asked.

I shot Junior an angry glance.

He gave a guilty smile. "Man, he was up in that joint hitting high notes like Maxwell! If some AR's or talent execs would'da been in there, they would'da signed him on the spot."

"Wwhhaatt?" Vito drawled, raising an eyebrow.

The cat was out of the bag and I couldn't put it back in. So, I admitted the truth. "I can do a lil' something."

Mike looked like he couldn't believe his ears. "What? Man, I knew this nigga since we was twelve and I never heard a hum. Now you tellin' me this nigga is R. Kelly?"

"Singing where it's at, brah. Them niggas get all the pussy," Vito grinned, giving a gold toothed smile.

"Don't forget about poets," Junior cut in. "We get it in, too."

"So, hit a note, nigga," Mike said, putting me on the spot. "Let us hear them pipes."

"Not right now, man. Some other time," I deflected.

"If heaven was here, that nigga would turn into Tank," Junior joked, jumping off the bench and mimicking me at the open mic.

94

"Who is Heaven?" Vito asked.

Before I could speak, Junior answered. "Y'all remember shorty he was freaking with on the dance floor when he went out with us? Light skinned with the phatty."

I watched the lights go on in Vito and Mike's eyes. "I asked you if you was hittin' that, ol' lyin' ass nigga!" He yelled, pushing me playfully.

"Wait, you gettin' pussy?" Vito asked. "I thought you was on that celibate shit, bruh?"

All eyes were on me, waiting for me to speak. "Man, it ain't like that. I ran into her at the open mic spot, and we kicked it a lil' bit."

"Nah, y'all. Rob lying. Keep it hot, nigga. You cuffed her up at the bar. Was singing to her n-shit," Junior embellished.

I shook my head.

"So, what's good, Rob? Is you keepin' her?" Vito asked.

Chapter 13

Heaven

I sighed heavily as I sat down on the couch and grabbed my laptop. It was time to get back to work. I went on Facebook and picked up where I left off, scrolling the profile pictures of suggested friends, looking for a familiar face. This had become a ritual for me. It was how I found most of my possible baby daddies. Sometimes it felt like my efforts were pathetic and downright trifling. I hated every moment of it and often wanted to give up the search. But then my motherly instincts kicked in and I pressed on. My boys' health depended on my perseverance.

As I scrolled the profiles, I began to think about the years I spent in the streets running wild. It was crazy of me to sleep with all those people. When I kicked it with my so-called friends, we used to brag about how many people we slept with. Back then it was something to be proud of. Today, I realized how stupid and degrading it was. What the hell was I thinking about? The question was rhetorical. I knew why I did it. I was broken, hurt, and lonely. Searching for acceptance with the wrong crowd. Trying to escape my past. The insane part about it all was that I repeated my past mistakes all over again every time I slept with another man or woman. Waking up next to a stranger was a constant reminder of the world I was trying to escape. So, I needed more Patrón, more pills, more weed, and more dope to push it all aside and continue destroying myself.

My phone vibrating on the table pulled me from thoughts of my self-destructive past. I looked at the screen and felt the butterflies as soon as I read the name. Tidbits of some of the conversations we had flashed in my head. I liked him a lot. He was funny, spiritual, strong, smart, driven, confident, and handsome. And his swagger was starting to grow on me. The problem was, I made a fool of myself the last time I was in his presence. I was a mess the last time I seen him at Starbucks. The combination of Majora dying and the emotional rollercoaster caused by my period had me acting crazy. Not to mention he made me nervous. I wondered how he would react if he knew my past. And it was then that I realized I hadn't answered the phone.

"Hello?"

"If I could hear your voice in the mornings before I said my prayers, I might skip them."

Hearing those words made my insides get warm. If someone had taken a picture of the smile spreading across my face, they could've sent it to Crest to be in their next commercial. "Hey, Robert. How have you been?"

"I guess I'm okay."

"What's going on? Are you okay?"

"Nah, not really. I have a problem that I need to run by you."

Oh no! He sounded serious. Please, Lord, don't let this be bad. "Go on. I'm listening," I said, trying to hide the worry in my voice.

"Ever since I sang at Tanna's, this strong desire to sing and write songs has come over me. I was trying to write today but I'm stuck. Figured I'd call you to see if you could help me. I want you to be the inspiration for my next song."

I didn't know how to react to what he said. I was flattered. "Uh, okay. Sure. What do you need me to do?"

"I want to see you. Let me take you out."

Wasn't expecting him to say that. I tried to think of an excuse, but the truth was, I wanted to see him too. But I didn't know if I could trust myself to be alone with him. He made me nervous. "My kids and little brother are home. I can't leave them alone."

"I know. I thought about that. Just give me the word and I'll come to you."

"Um... I don't know. It's not that easy for me. My kids have never seen me with a man. Except the day you were here. And I had a hard time explaining that. And Ray is another issue. He tries to be my man and my daddy. If you come over, I'll have to argue with him about it and I don't feel like going through no drama tonight."

"You know, normally that would've been enough to make me fall back. The last thing I wanna do is start trouble. But I can't take no for an answer. My desire to see you is no longer a want. It's a need. I'm not trying to sleep with you tonight, Heaven. I just want to be in your presence. And I'm not accepting no."

Wow. My heart did a back flip and landed in my throat, leaving me speechless. I'd heard similar words before, but I never believed them. Until now. "I don't know, Robert. Its—"

"Do you want to see me?" He cut in.

I decided to be honest. "I do. But I don't bring just anybody around my kids and Ray."

"Good thing I'm not just anybody." He laughed.

"Seriously, Robert. I think you're cool, but my family is important to me."

"I hear you, Heaven. And I understand. Look, I'm not proposing to you or anything, but I want to be around for the long haul. Not just tonight, tomorrow, or next week. I want to get to know you and your family. I really like you and I'm willing to do whatever it takes to be able to see you."

My insides were melting along with my defenses. "You're making this really hard, Robert," I whined.

"I'll tell you what, Heaven. How about you the three men in your life decide if you should have a fourth. I'll take you all out. To Dave and Busters. Then we'll leave it up to the boys to decide if I should see you again."

I didn't have any words left to fight with. "Okay, Robert. You win."

"It's not about winning or losing, Heaven. It's about living and making new friends. And new memories. I'll see you in a little while."

After he hung up, I stared at the phone in a little daze. Robert was smooth. He had worked his way past all of my defenses and now he was inside. I just hoped I wasn't making another mistake. After snapping out of my zone, I went to find the boys. I could hear their screams from Ray's room. When I opened the door, all three of them were sitting on the bed, video game joysticks in their hands, faces glued to the TV on the wall.

"Hey. What y'all up to?"

"Mama, they keep killing me," Jason whined, his thumbs rapidly pressing the buttons on the Xbox controller.

"I told him to be on my team, but he wanna be with the enemy," Ray said, his eyes never leaving the screen.

I decided to give them the news in small doses. "Hey, y'all wanna go to Dave and Busters?" I might as well had asked them if they wanted a million candy bars. Eyes popped, joysticks dropped, and I was mobbed.

"Yeah!"

"I wanna go!"

"Can we leave now?"

"Yeah, we will leave in a few minutes. Go get dressed."

The twins disappeared like they were animated cartoons, leaving a white trail of smoke behind as they raced to their room. Ray turned for his closet. I decided to give him the rest of the news.

"My friend is coming to pick us up."

"Reesy coming, too? Ooh, I hope Jody coming." He smiled while fumbling through his t-shirts. Jody was one of Reesy's daughter. Her and Ray were the same age and he had a giant crush on her. I felt kind of bad that I was about to crush his hopes of seeing her.

"I wasn't talking about Reesy."

Ray stopped going through the closet, turning to face me. "What friend? I thought Reesy was the only friend you had."

"This is a different friend. Robert. He was over here a couple months ago."

The wrinkles between his eyebrows got deeper as he frowned. "You talking about dude with white car?"

"Yeah. Him."

"I thought you didn't wanna see him no more."

"I ran into him a little while ago and we talked. He's okay. Nothing like the men in my past. Even Reesy likes him."

If there was anybody that knew everything about me, it was Ray. Most people only knew my good, but he knew my bad and ugly. I didn't hide anything from him. He knew what I was and what I was trying to become.

"Alright. But let me be the judge of that," he said before turning back to his closest.

I spun to leave when Ray spoke again.

"Ohh! And hope he drive that car again. That mug was tight!"

Chapter 14

Robert

It took me a little longer than I wanted, but with the help of my GPS, I was able to find Heaven's house. I walked upon the porch, noticing things about the house that I didn't notice the last time I was over. Like the bushes that lined the front or the awning that hung over the picture window. After taking in my surroundings, I pressed the doorbell.

"Who is it?" A deep male voice called from inside. Must be Ray, I figured.

"It's Robert."

The heavy oak door swung open and behind the screen was a big light skinned teenager. He had dark eyes and wavy black hair. We were the same height but he outweighed me by forty or fifty pounds. He wore a burgundy Rock Nation fit with retro Jordan's.

"What's up, man? Heaven here?" I asked, smiling extra wide to put the youngster at ease. "Yeah. Come in," he answered, eyeing me suspiciously and playing the 'I might be young but I'm the man in this house' role.

"You Ray, right?" I asked, keeping the conversation flowing as I stepped in the house.

"Yeah," he said, locking the door. "You Robert?"

I extended my hand. "Yeah. It's nice to meet you, lil' brah."

He gave a firm handshake. "Nice to meet you, too. Hold on. I'ma go get Heaven."

I looked around the living room, noticing the tabletops and walls were a few pictures of Heaven, the twins, and Ray. There was also a silver twelve-inch cross hanging on the wall above the sofa. What I didn't see was a TV. Only a laptop computer sitting on the table. After wiping my Nike boots off on the door mat, I walked around to look at the pictures. The one that caught my eye was a younger picture of Ray. He

looked to be about eight or nine and wore a football uniform.
Seeing the big teenager as a little kid was funny. I turned to
look at another picture when a piece of paper next to the
laptop caught my eye. I'm not the nosey type and I always try
to respect people's privacy, but three letters at the top of the
page made me take a closer look. DNA. I peeped around
before picking up the paper and scanning it quickly. Laron
Landry was given a paternity test for Mason. The results
came back negative. I hurriedly put the paper back where I
got it, but the damage had been done. Heaven didn't know
who fathered her children. I was beyond shocked. She didn't
seem like the type. But none of them did. Before I could
finish wrapping my mind around the results, I heard
footsteps coming into the living room. It was Ray.

"She said she a be out in a minute."

"Aight. No problem." I nodded. Problem was, there
was a huge problem. Two of them. The DNA results had
totally changed my impression of Heaven. What type of
woman didn't know who fathered her kids?

"Man, I love going to Dave and Busters," Ray was
saying. "I like that..."

I tuned the teenager out as my mind was sieged by new
revelations into Heaven's character. I wondered if she lied to
Laron like Sapphire lied to me? Making him believe he was
the boys' father when she knew all along that he wasn't. The
twins were five. It was a little late for paternity tests. I
wondered how many men she tested. Was she a hoe out to get
a trick? Was I the trick? Was the celibate story just a sham?
Was she really the woman that took me to her bed the first
night? Was everything I knew about her one big lie? What
else was she lying about?

"What kinda car was that you drove last time? How big
was them wheels?" Ray asked, his words penetrating my
thoughts.

"Uh, a Chevelle. On twenty sixes. That's my baby."
After the words left my lips, I wondered how many tricked
out cars he'd seen parked out front of the house.

"So, what are your intentions for my sister?" Ray
asked, flipping the script and becoming serious.

I paused to think of an answer. Ten minutes ago, I
thought the world of Heaven and wanted to bring her to meet
my parents. Now I wasn't sure if I even wanted to be seen in
public with her. "I, um, don't really have any intentions for
your sister. I just want to take y'all out and have a good time."

While I was answering the question, the twins came
shuffling into the living room and sat next to Ray. They all
watched me intently. It felt like I was on a job interview.

"Do you got kids?" Ray continued.

"Nah. No kids."

"Do you go to church?" One of the twins asked."

"Every Sunday."

"Are you trying to play my sister?"

I frowned at the question. She was the one playing the
games. But before I could answer, Heaven walked into the
living room and stole the words from my mouth. She wore a
form fitting gray turtleneck sweater, a pair of black jeans that
molded to her hips and thighs like a second skin, and furry
winter boots. I got stuck checking out her curves and had to
snatch my eyes away to look in those sparkling gray eyes.
She looked better every time I seen her.

"Sorry to keep you waiting. You know how girls are."
She giggled.

"It's cool. Ray and the twins were keeping me
company," I managed, struggling to keep my eyes locked
onto hers.

"What? You don't like this?" She asked, spinning
around so I could see every angle of her curvy body. She had
mistaken the struggle to keep my eyes focused as a sign that I
didn't like her clothes.

"Nah, you good, Heaven. You look really good," I complimented, wondering if she had done the twirl to entice me. She was a real vixen and I had to be careful. I was on to her game. And I was going to play it.

"Thank you," she blushed before turning to her family. "Grab your coats and let's go."

After everyone grabbed their coats, we set out for my Regal.

"Man, I wish you would've drove the other car," Ray said from the backseat.

"Snow and salt kills paint jobs, lil bro. I don't got five Gs to spend every summer to get a new paint job."

"Besides, everybody does not want to be the center of attention all the time," Heaven added. "Sometimes you have to keep a low profile."

I gave a sly side eye. What did she know about keeping a low profile? Is that how she tricked men? Pretending to be a celibate Christian and acting like she didn't want attention? Damn, she was good.

When we got to Dave and Busters, the twins ran around the place like they were on sugar highs. Ray eased up from being Heaven's protector and let his inner big kid out. I got in on the fun and chased the twins around and beat Ray in a couple rounds of Mortal Kombat before Heaven grabbed my attention. We ended up on a pair of stationary motorcycles and did some racing. I let her win a race or two.

"You know something, Robert? You're pretty cool. You can't race motorcycles, but you're cool," she bragged while climbing from the bike.

"I let you win. Don't get cocky. I'm trying to be a gentleman."

"Whatever! I won three in a row. You lost. I won," she teased, sticking her tongue out.

"Let's go again. One more race. I'ma smoke you," I challenged.

"You know what, Robert? All of a sudden, I feel tired," she yawned.

"For real? You not gon' give me a rematch?"

She laughed. "I think I'm gonna take my winning ways over to our table and sit down."

"Scary cat."

After going to check on Ray and the twins, we went back to the table to chill.

"Tell me more about you, Robert," Heaven said, staring into my soul with those bright gray eyes.

"What else do you want to know?" I asked, wondering if I should ask her to tell me more about herself. Specifically, who was the twins' father.

"I don't know. Surprise me. How much bad boy do you have in you? Ever been locked up?" I hesitated.

She noticed. "Oh my God! You were in jail?" She blurted, her eyes wide.

"I've done some time," I mumbled, not really wanting to go into that part of my life.

"You don't look like the type. I thought you graduated from college. I was just fishing with that question. I didn't expect it to be true."

"Yeah. Everything ain't always what it seems." *You should know that better than anybody*, I added in my head.

"I'm not judging. Everyone makes mistakes. Plus, you're different. Motivational speaking and welding. You're a true testament to the transforming power of God."

I didn't know how to respond. She was saying and doing all the right things but I couldn't shake that negative paternity result. I wanted to know why she wasn't showing signs of being upset after finding the results of a very important test. How could she be sitting across from me acting like everything was all good?

"Yeah, God is amazing. He has brought me through some stuff and helped me overcome some pretty big obstacles. Don't know where I would be without Him. So, what about you? It's your turn to share. Tell me more about you. How much bad girl do you have in you?"

She looked away. To me, that was as good as confessing that she had done something wrong. Apparently, she had a lot of bad girl in her. So much that she was ashamed. When she looked back at me, regret shown on her face and in her eyes.

"God has brought me through so much. When I think of everything he brought me through, I'm amazed that I'm still alive. His grace and mercy kept me. Gave me my babies. I'm just trying to be a better person for them. So, to answer your question, this good girl kicked all of the bad girl out. I don't smoke or drink. Last time I drank... You happened."

When she finished speaking, her beautiful face was flushed with regret and sadness. And something else. It looked like shame. I wanted to know more about why she was surprised to still be alive but the sad demeanor kept the questions at bay. Even though I was suspicious and curious about her, the last thing I wanted to do was make her uncomfortable or make her cry.

"Our greatest glory is not in never failing, but in rising every time we fall."

"Wow. That was good. And true. Where did you get that?"

I laughed.

"What's funny?" She frowned.

"I read that while I was in prison."

She laughed with me. And for the next couple of hours, we stayed away from each other's past, playing video games with the kids and enjoying each other's company. We left Dave and Busters at ten o'clock. As soon as Ray and the twins hopped in the backseat, they fell asleep. J Cole's music played softly as I drove. Thoughts of Heaven's past jumped into my head and wouldn't leave. She was good and bad. Sweet and sour. But she had a past. How deep were those secrets? How many skeletons were buried in her closet?

"Thank you, Robert."

I took my eyes from the road to glance at her. She was staring at me and smiling. "What are you talking about?"

"Thanks for taking me and my clan out and for allowing me to breathe again. I haven't had this much fun in a long time. So, thanks for showing me there are still good guys out there."

I held her stare for a moment. I was looking for signs of a lie or some type of game playing. Manipulation. Something. Anything. But the eyes that stared back at me were sincere. Truthful. But I couldn't shake those DNA results.

"No problem. You have a good family," I said weakly.

She picked up on the tone. "What's wrong, Robert?"

"Nothing."

She spun to face me, laying her back against the door. "So you mean to tell me that you've been laughing and having a good time with us all night and now that something is bothering you, which I can see is, you won't tell me?"

I tried to think of a lie, but the only thing that came to mind was those DNA results. "I seen the DNA results for the twins."

I kept my eyes mostly on the road but watched her out of my peripheral. A mixture of emotions spread across her face. Anger. Embarrassment. Hurt. Shame. Then nothing. She spun in the seat, facing forward, watching the road with me. Her face didn't show any emotion and she stopped talking. Neither of us said a word for almost a full minute.

"I don't know why I thought you were different," she mumbled. "Quick to judge, like everybody else. Like you don't have a past. Like you don't have secrets."

Her words were packed with emotion and they cut me. Made me think of the secrets I held while professing to be a celibate Christian. "I'm sorry, Heaven. I didn't mean to snoop. Or judge. I wish I didn't see it. I wish it wasn't bothering me, but it is."

She turned to me, her gray eyes changing to silver as they blazed with anger. "So, what now? You think I'm some hoe? You think I'm lying to you and trying to play you?"

She asked the questions as if she was reading my mind. And when I didn't respond quick enough, the fire in her eyes blazed hotter.

"Silence don't lie, Robert."

After feeding me the line, silence filled the car. I began to feel like a piece of trash when she began sniffling and wiping tears from her eyes. I wanted to comfort her but I didn't know what to say. Then, she put on a mask. It looked stoic and impenetrable. At that point, I knew she shut down so I didn't even bother trying to apologize. When I pulled onto her block, she turned to the backseat and shook Ray.

"Get up, Ray. We're home. Grab Mason."

"I can help," I tried.

"I don't want you to help me. We got it."

I wanted to say something else, but I knew the words would be a useless waste of breath. Her body language and words told me she hated me. I didn't want to make it worse.

"Aight, Robert," Ray nodded. "I got that new Special Ops. Next time you come over, I'ma beat you down. Plus, I need my rematch in Mortal Kombat."

"Yeah, man. Imma see you later. For sure. Bye, Heaven."

She acted like she didn't hear me, slammed the door and walked away. Damn.

Chapter 15

Heaven

Four days had gone by since my date with Robert and I missed him. And that surprised me because I had never missed a man before. I've never met a man that gave me a reason to miss him. Plus, I barely knew him. We had been in each other's presence only a hand full of times but in that short time, I discovered everything that I wanted in my future husband. He was fun, funny, confident, smart, and a whole bunch of other things that I adored. The date was great and my kids and brother had already asked about him coming over again. He slid right into my life as easily as a knife through warm butter. But then he had to reveal the jerk side of him. He snooped through my things and invaded my privacy. That was wrong on so many levels. Was he trustworthy? Was he a stalker? Then, he formed a negative opinion of me and judged me. That pissed me off more than him finding the DNA test because I thought he seen me for me and for the person I was today. I was hoping that he could be the one I could let down my guard with.

"Did Robert call you yet?" Ray asked, appearing from the hallway.

"No. I told you he was out of town." I didn't want to tell him or the twins that we stopped talking.

"Oh yeah. I forgot. Aight, when he call, tell him I said, what up?"

"I got you."

I shook my head when Ray walked away. If I didn't know any better, I would've swore he liked Robert more than I did. But I understood how he felt. That was the only male friend of mine that he had ever spent time with. Plus, Robert was cool and had a bunch of likeable qualities. When my phone began vibrating on the table, my stomach did a flip and I hoped I had spoken him up. When I grabbed the phone and seen Reesy's name, I felt let down. "Hey, Reesy," I answered weakly.

"What's wrong, love? He still didn't call you?" She asked, instantly picking up on my mood and the cause of it.

"No. I'm starting to think that he won't. It's been four days."

"Well, if he doesn't, that's his loss. You are a beautiful woman on the outside and inside. If he allows your past to change his opinion of you or how he feels, then he's not the one for you."

"I should've gotten rid of those results. I don't even know why I kept them."

"Oh no, Heaven. Don't go blaming yourself. It's not your fault. He was being nosey and invading your privacy. That's a red flag right there. You know what they say about people who go looking for stuff. Normally, they find it. Now he has to decide if he can accept what he found. None of that is your fault. He shouldn't have snooped in your business. What is he, some kind of stalker or something? Who does that?"

"Yeah, you're right. I guess I just liked him a lot. I've never been so infatuated with somebody so quick. I know I'm not in love with him. I'm sure of that. I could go on living the rest of my life without ever seeing him again and be fine. But at the same time, knowing it's possible that I might not talk to him again makes me feel some kind of way."

"I get it, love. But just know... wait. Hold on. I think Tommy just put a hole in my wall. Let me call you back, sweety."

She hung up the phone before I could say bye. I threw my phone on the couch and thought about what Reesy said. If my past changes the way he sees or thinks about me, then maybe he wasn't the one for me. She was right. If a man couldn't accept me for me, then he didn't deserve me. I shouldn't have to hide my past. Either they would accept it or wouldn't. After talking myself out of the woe is me attitude, I decided to do something to take my mind off of Robert. I walked over to my purse and pulled out the card Lay-Lay sent me. There was a beautiful drawing on the cover of a stork carrying a set of twin babies in a basket. On the inside he left a short message: "Sorry about the results. If you ever need a friend, I'm here. Lay-Lay." I took the card over to my laptop and began typing my final letter to him.

Dear Lay-Lay, Thank you for the card. It is beautiful and made me smile. I'm sorry about the paternity results, too. I wanted this search to be over so badly. But it is what it is. This isn't my first time going through this and probably won't be my last. Thank you for being so understanding. You are a good man. Unfortunately, this will be my last letter to you. I have a busy life and too much responsibility to try to nurture a friendship with you while you're in there. Thank you for the kind letters. I appreciated everything you wrote to me and I enjoyed getting to know you better. I hope that you get out here soon and enjoy life and freedom. Take care of yourself.

Always and forever, Heaven.

After rereading the letter to check for errors, I printed it off and stuck it in an envelope. I was sealing the letter shut when Mason stumbled into the living room.

"Mommy, I don't feel good," he moaned.

I looked up from sealing the envelope and seen my son's face and clothes were covered in blood. His skin was pale as a ghost's and he looked like he was about to topple over at any moment. The sight was terrifying. I'd seen a similar sight two years ago when I found out my kids had lymphocytic leukemia.

"Mason, what happened, baby?" I called, dropping the letter and rushing to him.

Before I could get there, his eyes rolled to the back of his head and he collapsed.

"Nooooo!" I screamed, kneeling beside him. "Mason! Mason, wake up!" I shook him but he didn't wake up.

"Ray, call 911! Hurry up!" I called, lifting Mason from the floor and carrying him to the bathroom. "Mason! Mason, wake up baby!" I called as I wet a towel with cold water and began wiping the blood from his face.

His eyes fluttered again but they didn't open.

"What happened?" Ray asked, appearing in the bathroom doorway. When he seen Mason, his eyes grew wide with shock and fear.

"He fainted. Hurry up and call an ambulance! Hurry up!"

Chapter 16

Robert

"We all have a past, son. Even you," my mom said, giving me that motherly look. "Does she know why you went to prison? Does she know about Roger? What about Sapphire? Have you told Heaven about her and the boys?"

I looked away from the phone and up to Vito's empty front porch. I was sitting outside of his house finishing the conversation with my mother on Facetime. "No, I haven't told her about none of that. That stuff is different."

Moms gave me the stupid face. "How so?"

"Because I don't got five year old twins with no daddy"

"That's not fair, Robert. The point isn't that she has kids and doesn't know who their father is. The point is you have a shady past just like she does. You should have asked her about the situation instead of forming an opinion and judging her. How do you feel when people who don't know you judge you because you've spent five years in prison? I know it doesn't feel good because you've told me. If you can change, why can't she? You're the pot calling the kettle black when you're just as black. You are keeping your secrets but expecting her to spill all of hers on the first date. That's not right and you know it."

I was silent for a moment. Everything she said made perfect sense. "I just don't want to get into another Sapphire situation."

"From what you told me, she doesn't sound anything like that manipulating, lying Jezebel. Heaven's been celibate for five years. She's a Christian. You're the only man that's ever been around her kids. She has a job but wants more. To me, she sounds like a good woman and good mother. But she has a past. And it might be ugly. But whose isn't? I love your father with all of my heart but I still haven't told him about some of the things I've been through. And it's not because I don't trust him, because I do. I just don't want him to see all my skeletons. And a part of me doesn't want to face some of those demons."

Hearing my mother break everything down gave me an epiphany. In that moment, everything became clear and made sense. I had secrets too. And some of them were locked away tighter than Fort Knox. "I got it, ma. I hear you."

She smiled. "Good. I have to get going. Call her."

"Okay, ma. Bye."

"Wait, Robert!" She called, stopping me from hanging up.

"Yeah."

"Trust is earned, not given. Remember that. If she does decide to tell you about her past, don't judge her by it. Judge her by the woman she is today, not by her short comings. We've all fallen short, and that is not a bad thing. Falling short and failing teaches us what not to do and how to succeed."

After ending the call with my mom, I let her wise words bounce around my head. Heaven had revealed herself to be a celibate Christian, a good mother, and a strong and loving sister. She was a talented poet with a heart of gold. She was fine without conceit. Funny, smart, and compassionate. And she did have a past. The celibacy was the giveaway. I had become 'kind of celibate' because sex complicated my life and sometimes got me into trouble. I had more in common with Heaven than different. When I finished collecting my thoughts, I hopped out the car and walked up Vito's freshly shoveled walkway. Mike texted me to come over because It was 'really important' with all kinds of funny emojis. I walked upon the porch and gave the door a few knocks.

"Who dat?" Vito asked.

"Robert. Open the door, fool. Its cold out here!"

When the door opened, Vito was standing in the doorway smiling a gold toothed smile. "What's hannin, dawg? Come in. Er'body up in here."

I stepped in the house and seen Mike and Junior sitting on the couch drinking beers. On another couch was a female I'd never seen before. She was kind of cute in a plain sort of way. Dark skin, long phony ponytail, and it looked like she was packing a few extra pounds. What got my attention were her eyes. They were polite, but I could tell she had seen some things.

"What's good?" I nodded to my boys.

Mike jumped up and headed for me quickly. "Sup, dawg?" He wrapped me in a hug and began whispering in my ear. "Dawg, that's Vito new girl," he snickered.

I didn't know what to do or say. If I looked at her, she would know we were talking about her. So, instead of acknowledging her, I greeted Junior "Poetry God, what's good?"

"What's up, Rob?"

"Rob, let me introduce you to Queesha," Vito said. "Queesha, this my nigga, Rob."

Mike bust out laughing again. Literally fell against the wall and thrashed around like he was having a stroke. We all looked at him like he was crazy before I turned to the woman.

"What's up, Queesha? Nice to meet you."

"Nice to meet you too, Robert," she said in a voice filled with southern twang. But her accent wasn't the problem. The gold teeth were. She had more gold in her mouth than Vito. Six on the top row and six on the bottom row. My startled reaction to her grill had Mike in tears.

"You see the comedian over there," Vito said, mugging Mike.

I tried as best as I could to hold in my laughter but Mike's antics were making it hard.

"Hold up, dawg! Hold up," Mike breathed, trying to catch his breath and wiping tears from his eyes. "She got more gold teeth than you, my nigga! I bet when y'all in bed and smile at night, the whole room light up like y'all gotta disco ball in that bitch!" Mike cracked, busting out laughing again.

The joke was weak but the way he was throwing himself around the room made it funny and I lost the battle with holding my laugh.

"So, you juss gon' let yo niccas clown me like dat, Vito?" Queesha asked, getting an attitude.

"C'mon, Mike. Chill that shit, nigga," Vito said too little too late.

"Nah, dis nicca been clownin' me since I got here and you just now sayin' sumthin'. Either he out or I am."

A hush fell over the living room when she gave the ultimatum. Vito let out a grunt and shook his head. He knew the code. The bros came first, unless she was wifey.

"So dat's how it is, Vito?" Queesha asked angrily, shooting to her feet.

And that's when I seen her booty. It was gigantic! Deserved its own orbit. Should've been in the book of world records. Easily the biggest booty I had ever seen in my life. Now I understood why Vito didn't care about all her gold teeth.

"Cmon, Queesha. He ain't mean it," Vito said, trying to calm her.

"Fuck you and yo' niccas. I'm out dis bitch!" She cursed, her booty thunder clapping in the spandex as she power walked towards the front door.

"Cmon, baby! Don't leave," Vito called as he gave chase.

Junior shot Mike a disappointed look and shook his head. "You went too far, fam."

"What? You the one tripping. Shit I ain't going far enough," Mike mugged. "I ain't finna let my nigga go out like that. Shorty gotta big booty, but he can do better. You niggas know she just finished doing eight years for killing her baby daddy? My nigga ain't finna go out like that."

"She killed her baby daddy?" I asked, surprised by the revelation. Vito was a player and I definitely didn't want him dealing with a chick that could kill.

"But that's on him. He can mess with or date whoever he wants. He grown," Junior argued.

"Nah, brah. Mike right on this," I said. "If we see one of us doing something that could get us in a jam, we gotta speak up."

"Thank you, Rob," Mike said. "Vito is my nigga and I ain't finna let him get blinded by no big booty."

I was about to jump in again but my phone started ringing. When I seen Heaven's name on the screen, my mind went blank. A symphony of thoughts and emotions flooded my body as I answered. "Hello?"

"Robert, I think my nephew dead!" Ray yelled in a panicked voice.

I felt a little pain in my chest. "What do you mean he dead? What happened?"

"We at Children's Hospital. Heaven told me to call you. He was bleeding and wasn't moving. I think he dead," Ray cried.

I don't know why, but I felt connected to the injured little boy. I tore up out of Vito's house like the police were rushing through the back door and I had a backpack full of drugs. I jumped in the Regal and sped away. Heaven wasn't my girl, Mason wasn't my son, and I barely knew Ray, but I rushed to the hospital to be with them. I was speeding through a yellow light when my phone rang. It was Junior

"What's good, bro?" I answered.

"What's up with you, nigga? Why you run up outta here like that? You good?"

"Yeah. Heaven son in the hospital. They think he dead or something."

"What? Damn, brah! You need us to be there with you?"

"Nah, I got it. I'ma holla at you later on."

When I got to Children's Hospital, I found Ray in the waiting room. He looked a mess. Eyes red, clothes wrinkled, and blood spots on his pants.

"What's up, man? Where is your sister?"

"She with Mason and the doctors. They told us to wait out here."

"Is that his blood? How is he?"

"I don't know. He wasn't moving, man."

"Where's Jason?" I asked when I noticed the other twin missing.

"Reesy took him to the bathroom."

As I looked Ray over, I noticed he lost all the bravado and coolness he displayed the last time I'd seen him. Now he looked like a scared little boy inside a man's body. And I understood.

"He's going to be alright, man," I said, reaching out to wrap an arm around the teenager's wide shoulders.

We sat down and began the nervous wait for news on Mason's condition. There were a couple more families in the waiting room wearing the same grim expressions that we wore. About five minutes later, Reesy showed up with Jason. She looked surprised to see me.

"Hey, Robert. I wasn't expecting to see you here."

"Ray called and told me about Mason. How is he?"

Reesy cut her eyes at Ray before responding. "I don't know. By the time I got here, they were already in the back. I haven't talked to Heaven yet. Have you?"

"No. I just got the call from Ray that she wanted me to come so I came. I said a prayer for him on the way. I hope the little dude is okay."

"That's all we can do is leave it in God's hands," Reesy said, shooting Ray another glance. We all sat and began the long wait for information. During the wait, I thought about my own brother. Roger died way too young. It saddened me a little to know that there was a chance that Jason may grow up to have these same thoughts and feelings. And I was caught up in those thoughts when Heaven emerged from a set of double doors across the room. She looked stressed and her purple sweat suit was covered in blood. When her eyes found mine, she looked surprised.

"Mommy! Mommy, is my brother okay?" Jason asked as he ran to her.

She picked up the toddler and said something to him that the distance wouldn't allow me to hear. I stood with Ray, and Reesy as she walked over.

"How is he?" Reesy asked.

"He's okay. The Leukemia is getting more aggressive. They stabilized him and are giving him medicine," she explained. "They want to keep him overnight and I'm staying. Will you keep Ray and Jason?"

"You don't even have to ask, love. I got them," Reesy said.

Then, Heaven turned to me. I could see questions floating in her eyes. "What are you doing here?"

I was surprised by the question. "Ray called and said you wanted me to come."

She frowned. The look said that she didn't tell Ray to call me. We all turned to Ray. He shifted nervously under the adult stares.

"I was scared. Plus, I knew something was wrong with you and Robert. I wanted to fix it. Robert is cool, sis. Sorry," Ray apologized, going into his pocket and giving Heaven back her phone.

An awkward silence fell upon us. "C'mon, y'all. Let's go get some ice cream sundaes," Reesy said, grabbing Jason from Heaven's arms.

"Thanks, Reesy. I'll call you later," Heaven said.

I stood and watched Reesy walk away with the boys. Before they went outside, Ray turned and gave me a sly smile. My mother's words began to play in my head. Heaven was a good woman.

"I'm sorry, Heaven," I blurted.

She looked up at me, confusion lighting her eyes. Her thoughts were conflicted. I let her figure out what she wanted to say.

"You don't have to be here. You don't have to apologize. I'm good."

"Yes, I have to apologize. I had no right to go through your things. I'm sorry. I shouldn't have done that. I don't normally do things like that. I respect people's privacy. And I shouldn't have judged you. I allowed ghosts from my own past to cloud my thinking. I was wrong."

I could see her weighing my words.

"I accept your apology, Robert. But that doesn't change what you think of me. I seen it in your face. In your eyes. In your silence."

"No, Heaven. I don't think of you how you think I do. I mean, I did back then, but that was because I was shocked. You don't look like you have problems. You don't walk around with your problems on your sleeve. So I was surprised and I handled it wrong. But we all have a past. We all have secrets. We all are running from something. We all have things that we hide from people because we don't want to be judged by them. I'm no different. I understand, Heaven. And it's okay."

She searched my eyes for the truth. I met and held her stare.

"So, what exactly are you saying, Robert?"

"I'm not saying anything. I just want to be able to kick it with you again. Laugh again. Have fun. And whatever your pain, whatever your hurt, whatever your secrets, you can keep them as long as you want. But just know that how I feel about you is bigger than all the bad and embarrassing things that you've ever been through."

"Mmmm Mmmhhh!"

The noise came from somewhere to my left. It sounded like whoever made the sound had just tasted one of Patti Labelle's pies. I looked over and seen an older black woman watching me and Heaven like we were actors in her favorite movie. And when I looked around the waiting room, I seen the same looks from all the people present. When I turned back to Heaven, she looked embarrassed. I wanted her to say something. I liked her. Wanted her. Not only was she a beautiful woman, but her spirit captivated me. Her essence drove me wild. Just being in her presence made me feel good. I wanted her in every imaginable way. So I stood in that waiting room with all the other people waiting for her to speak.

"Girl, you better say something," the lady that made the noise spoke. "Cause if you don't want him, I'll take him."

That made Heaven smile. "C'mon," she said, grabbing my arm and leading me away.

Chapter 17

Heaven

My body was on fire!

It felt like someone had boiled a couple points of blood and fed it to my body through an IV. It wasn't a painful feeling but the exact opposite. I had never felt so alive! My skin was prickly, my scalp tingled, and my insides grew warm. Robert's words had awakened something deep inside of me. Something that I didn't even know was there. It felt like a first rain to a land that had been scorched by drought. As I dragged Robert through the hospital corridors, his words kept playing in my head. They were beautiful words. Healing words. Soul touching and emotion stirring words. Words I'd longed to hear. Needed to hear. And now I wanted to get him alone. I wanted him to see me. For him to know me. I wanted to know if his words were true. See if his feelings for me could really be bigger than my past. When we got to Mason's room, I led him inside and closed the door. I spun around, ready to tell him everything that I never had the courage or a reason to tell another man. But he wasn't focused on me. He was standing next to Mason's bed, care and compassion on his face. I walked over to stand next to him and we watched Mason sleep.

"You said he has Leukemia?" Robert asked.

"Yes. Him and Jason. They went through chemotherapy and radiation therapy last year. We thought it was gone. Then, they relapsed."

"What kind of Leukemia do they have?"

"It's called Acute Lymphocytic Leukemia. Their bone marrow is making abnormal white blood cells. It's harder for their bodies to fight off infections. Getting sick is dangerous for them. One time, they caught colds and it put them in the hospital for two weeks."

"That's messed up," he mourned.

I sat on the bed next to Mason and began caressing his face. "I hate seeing my kids in pain or sick and I can't do anything to help them. I feel so helpless sometimes," I mumbled, wiping away the tears that began to spill.

"You gotta keep praying and believing that God is going to work it out. What's the next step? Can they be cured?"

"Yes. They need a bone marrow transplant but me and Ray are not a match."

He nodded. "You need their father, huh?"

"Yes," I whispered.

We grew quiet. His words began to play in my head again. "Did you really mean what you said out there?"

"Every word."

We began an intimate staring contest. "Do you really think you can handle my past?"

"Can you handle mine?"

His question surprised me. The uncertainty in his eyes surprised me even more. He had secrets too.

"I hope so," I answered truthfully.

"Me too," he mumbled before sitting on the bed next to me.

I searched his eyes for a telltale sign on whether or not I could trust him. He seemed to know what I was doing because he grabbed my hand and held it, not saying a word. My intuition told me I could trust him. So I began.

"I never really knew my father. I mean, I knew his name was Mark Sorrentine, but I never knew him. I knew he was Italian, drove a nice car, liked to drink vodka, and that his jet black hair was always slicked to the back; but I never knew him. I don't know if I have any brothers and sisters, besides Ray. I never met anyone on his side of the family, or even knew if he had a family. And I never knew if he loved me.

Never heard him say it. Not once. Mark came around a couple times a month but never spoke to me much. Just the standard questions. How is school? How are my grades? Am I giving my mom any trouble? Then, him and mom would start drinking vodka. After they got drunk, they would disappear into her room. They would stay there for an hour or two. And after my mom finished screaming his name, he would leave."

"Right after I turned ten, he stopped coming around for good. I think it had something to do with my mother getting pregnant with Ray. I remember hearing them argue about a baby the last time he came over. Since I was ten and didn't see a baby in the house, I didn't know what was going on. Didn't put the pieces of the puzzle together until a few years later. So Ray never got the chance to meet him. Probably for the best."

"My father was the only man I ever seen my mother with, until she met Arthur. She brought him home to meet us when Ray was about one. I hated him from the moment I laid eyes on him. Something inside my young mind told me that he was no good. His tall, skinny, and lanky frame reminded me of a puppet with no strings. He had little beady eyes that made him look like he was always up to no good. And his breath stank. Like he was dying on the inside.

My mom never really had any self-esteem so any time a man that showed interest in her, she melted. Even if they didn't deserve her. Like Arthur. For the life of me, I can't figure out why my mom had a negative self-image of herself. To me, she was the most beautiful woman in the world. She was West Indian and Hmong. Long silky black hair. Beautiful brown skin. Sexy slanted eyes. Had she met the right people, she could've been a movie star or model. But she never got the chance. And when the drugs started, she checked out on life."

124

"Arthur had only been living with us for a couple of weeks when he introduced her to drugs. First, it was weed. They didn't even hide when they smoked. The weed changed to Cocaine. Cocaine led to crack. Crack led to heroin. The heroin is what took my mom from us. She gave up on me and Ray. All that mattered was getting high. By the time I was twelve, I was raising Ray and taking care of the house by myself. Not only did I have to wake myself, feed myself, and make sure I got to school on time, but I also had to cook, clean, do homework, and take care of Ray. When puberty kicked in, I wasn't the only one that noticed."

I paused to gather myself as I relived my past. Robert continued to hold my hand.

"I was thirteen they first time Arthur touched me. My mom was out getting drugs and Arthur was home with me and Ray. I was sitting at the kitchen table doing my homework when Ray started crying. I got up to make him a bottle of sugar water when Arthur walked in the kitchen. When I saw the look in his eyes, I knew something was up. He had been watching me and giving me these long crazy looks for a while. When I saw that look in his eyes, I tried to leave the kitchen but he stopped me. I tried to push past him, but he was too strong. He wrapped me up in his arms, spun me around and started grinding on my butt. *'You gon' be one fine lil bitch!'* he told me while squeezing my breasts. I screamed for him to let me go but he didn't. Instead, he spun me around and stuck his tongue in my mouth. His breath stank so bad that I threw up and he let me go. Then, he threatened me. Said if I told my mother what happened, he would kill her and Ray. I was scared of him and believed he would do like he said so I stayed quiet."

When the tears began spilling, I let them flow.

Robert squeezed my hand tightly. "It's okay, Heaven. You good. You don't, don't have to talk about it no more. "

I took a moment to get my tears under control before telling him some more. "As time went on, the abuse got worse. He went from feeling me up to sneaking into my room at night. He took my virginity. Just took it. Held his hand over my mouth and raped me while my mother slept in the other room. It hurt so bad that I thought he was killing me. By the time I turned fourteen, he was doing it three or four times a week. I didn't say anything to anyone. I believed his threats and thought I was protecting my family by giving him what he wanted. Then, one day I was in school and a rape survivor came to speak to us. She told her story and I cried. She told us to tell someone we trust if we ever got sexually assaulted.

That gave me the courage to finally tell my mother what he was doing to me. I knew she would protect me and kick him out. So when I got home from school, I told her everything. But my mom was too far gone. Said her man don't want no little girls and called me a liar. I cried and begged her to believe me. She responded by slapping me. Slapped me so hard that I fell on the ground. Then, she threatened to kill me if I ever told that lie again. That night while lying in my bed, I decided to run away. I didn't want to leave Ray, but I knew that I had to get out of that house if I wanted to survive. So I woke up the next morning like I was going to school and never went back home. Instead of books, I filled my book bag with clothes. I had no idea what life on the street would be like, but I knew it couldn't be any worse than my house."

"Nobody came to look for me. My mother never called the police or filed a missing report. It only took me about a week to figure out how to use my looks to get what I wanted. Everybody told me how beautiful I was, and almost every man that I walked by would look at my body. So in exchange for a place to sleep, money, food, clothes, drugs, or liquor, I gave them my body. Men, women, young, old, it didn't matter as long as they gave me what I wanted. I stopped counting how many people I slept with after fifty. I ran the streets for seven years, until I got pregnant. My kids literally saved my life. They are the reasons that I am the woman I am today. Them and Reesy. I met her on the way to get an abortion. I believe God sent her to me. She helped me get cleaned up, finish school, find a job, and best of all, she introduced me to Jesus. If it wasn't for her, my kids and the grace of God, I would be dead."

"She even helped me find Ray and get him from Child Protective Services. While I was running the streets, my mom died of an overdose. We didn't have any next of kin so they put him in the system. I don't even know when my mother died. I never went back home to check on her. I found out she was dead while standing in line buying diapers at Walmart. Someone my mom used to get high with told me. I don't even know if she had a funeral. Don't have anything to remind me of her. Not even a picture. It's almost like she never existed. And those DNA papers that you saw were for the sixteenth man that I've tested. I wanted to give up searching so many times, but I can't. My boys need me to find their father to see if he is a match for their bone marrow transplant. Otherwise, they will probably die."

Chapter 18

Robert

Listening to Heaven's story left me speechless. It was a true irony of life that someone so beautiful could have a past so ugly. After she finished talking, I held her while we watched Mason sleep. As I replayed her story in my head, I got angry. She didn't deserve the abuse. No child deserved to lose their virginity to a rapist. And it saddened me because I had heard the story before from some of the children that I spoke to after my motivational speeches. Little girls robbed of their innocence and forced to grow up too fast. Little boys that were neglected and molested, who would eventually grow up to be molesters, rapists, and killers. I wasn't going to judge Heaven, nor was I going to leave her. I wanted to heal her. Show her a side of a man different from her experiences.

At some point during the evening, I moved to the chair beside Mason's bed. The piece of furniture was soft and my body was mentally and emotionally drained. When the sleep came to get me, I didn't resist. Slept all night until I was awakened by the vibration from the 'other' phone in my pocket. I pulled it out and hit the power, not bothering to check the caller. I already knew who it was and what she wanted. And the way I was feeling, I probably wouldn't need the phone anymore.

"Kinda early for calls."

Heaven's voice startled me a little. I looked up and found her curled up in bed next to Mason.

"You still woke?" I asked, standing and stretching. My joints popped like small fireworks.

"I can't sleep knowing that my baby is hurting."

"He's going to be okay. I know it. He has your strength. Plus, we serve an amazing God."

She smiled. "So, why didn't you answer the phone?"

Her persistence about the phone call caught me off guard. I thought about telling a lie but she was giving me that *'don't you lie to me'* look. Like she knew a woman was trying to call me. So I sat back down in the chair and gathered my thoughts. Heaven didn't rush me. She remained quiet. Waiting.

"That was Sapphire."

She nodded. "You have a girlfriend?"

There was no easy way to describe who Sapphire was, so I started at the beginning. "She's not my girlfriend, but we do have a relationship. Just let me explain. I met her when we were sophomores at Marshall High School. Back then, Sapphire was the baddest girl in school and I was the star basketball player. You know how that goes. We started dating and eventually having sex. She was ahead of her time in the bedroom and I was a little wet behind the ears and got whipped. She was only the second girl I'd had sex with and she did it so good that my young body confused lust for love. Plans were made for the white house with the picket fence, two kids, and a dog after graduation."

"For me, graduation never came. I dropped out of school as a junior to hit the streets full time. Ended up in jail right after I turned twenty. I leaned on Sapphire for comfort and peace of mind during my time in the county jail. She held me down and promised she would wait for me. Swore that she would be my ride or die chick. Turned out, she would only ride or die when I was free. When the judge gave me five years, she broke. While locked up, I ran into some dudes I went to high school with. After we caught up, they always asked about Sapphire. I never questioned why they asked about her because I assumed they were just acknowledging that I had a bad one. It wasn't until I ran into this dude named Al Davis, an ex-teammate from our high school basketball team, that I would find out the truth. And the truth crushed me."

"Turns out Sapphire was a thot. The reason why Sapphire was so good at sex was because she got lots of practice. See, by the time we got to the eleventh grade, I was barely coming to school. The streets were calling me and slowly but surely I was answering. And while I was out grinding in the street, she was at school grinding on anybody and everybody.

Al told me about some of the parties they threw when they skipped school. Sapphire was always present. He told me how they would get her faded and then run trains on her. Said one time they had a line outside the bedroom door and she knocked them all down. I still remember the burning I felt in my chest when Al told me my high school sweetheart was a bust down. I knew she liked kinky sex but I thought it was all for me. Turned out, she was doing it for anyone that was ready and willing."

" I ended up doing the bid without hearing another word from her. By the time I got out, I was over her and ready to move on with my life. I left prison bigger and better, and my heart was a little colder. I had written a few business plans and became a certified welder while doing my time. I ditched the streets and everything that came along with them to put my plans into action. What I didn't plan on was running into Sapphire again. I had been out a month when I seen her in the grocery store. As soon as I seen her, all those feelings I thought I got out of my system came rushing back. I tried to stick to my guns about not letting her back in my life, but after a few apologies and confessions of love, I was back in her bed. Truth was, I hadn't met a woman that could do the things she could do sexually. She knew my body like she created me."

"I planned to keep our thing strictly sexual. No strings attached. She agreed. We met up a couple times a week and got it on. Things went well for about two months. Then, she

130

caught feelings. Started saying I was her man. I didn't take what she was saying too serious because I knew it wasn't official. All that changed when she seen me at the mall with my female cousin, Tae. Sapphire acted a fool. She thought my cousin was a girl I was sleeping with and went off. Didn't even give me a chance to explain. Just wilded out and tore up the store trying to fight me and Tae. I ended up in jail on a P.O hold. Had to sit thirty two days for them to finish the investigation and let me out. I spent all of those days pacing my cell cursing the day I ever met her. When I got out, the first thing I did was call Sapphire and break things off. She cried, begged me to give her another chance, and confessed her love. But this time I stuck to my guns. I was done. Cutting her off for good"

"But Sapphire was persistent. She showed up to my job and acted a fool. My boss had to call the police to make her leave. And when I went home later that night, she was outside my apartment building. Acted a fool there too. Other tenants started complaining to the building owner about her showing up at all times of the day and night screaming outside my window. Landlord kicked me out. After moving into a new place, my life was drama free. Lasted about eight or nine months. Ended up running into Sapphire at Grand Avenue Mall. When she seen me, she flipped her wig. And the only way she would chill was if I gave her my number. I did one better and bought a phone especially for her. This phone. And it's been this way for years."

Heaven took her time responding. "So, you've never been celibate?"

That wasn't the question I expected her to ask. "Yeah. I mean, nah. For like a month," I stuttered.

"You're such a liar, " she chuckled. "And you have a crazy one on your hands. If I was you, I probably would've moved out of town to get away from her crazy butt."

I couldn't believe that she took my lie about being celibate so well. "So, you not mad that I'm not celibate?"

"No. I'm a little disappointed, but I'm not mad. You said that you had a past. Now I know. So, Sapphire's stuff was really that good?"

I didn't know if there was a right or wrong answer the question so I told the truth. "Yeah. I guess so."

She smirked. "So when was the last time you seen her?"

"A couple weeks ago. The more time I spend with you, the less I want to see her."

Heaven laughed and rolled her eyes. "Whatever, Robert."

I didn't laugh. "I'm not playing, Heaven. I'm serious."

Her mood changed back to serious. "So, why do you still have that phone?"

Damn. That was a good question and I didn't have a good answer. So I responded the only way I could. I dug into my pocket and threw Sapphire's phone on the bed.

***

They kept Mason in the hospital for two weeks. The Leukemia had returned so he had to go through chemotherapy to kill the damaged white blood cells. Every day after I got off work, I went to the hospital and spent time with him and Heaven. We talked about anything and everything and there was never a dull moment. I enjoyed her company and a bond grew from all the time we spent together. I had never felt as close to any woman as I did Heaven. Not even Sapphire. And I never asked what she did with Sapphire's phone either. It didn't matter.

After climbing from the Regal, I walked in the hospital and made my way to the gift shop. Mason was being released today and I wanted to get him something to put a smile on his face. I searched the small shop for a few minutes before buying balloons and a teddy bear wearing nurse scrubs. After purchasing the gifts, I headed to the room. I walked in and seen Mason sitting in a wheelchair fully dressed. Heaven sat in the chair next to the bed talking to the doctor.

"Robert!" Mason yelled, climbing from the wheelchair and walking to me.

"Hey, lil man! I got this for you."

"Oh man! Thanks."

"Cmon, man. Let's get back in the wheelchair so we can get out of here," I said, before turning to the grown-ups. "Hey, Heaven. What's up, Doctor Newhouse? My lil Buddy ready to get up outta here?"

"Hi, Robert. Your little buddy is a fighter and he's ready to go. I was just going over a few things with Heaven," the doctor explained before turning back to Heaven. "While y'all finish talking, I'ma take Mason on a ride. We out! Hang on, lil buddy!" I said, pushing him from the room.

Mason laughed as we raced down the hallway. "Go faster, Robert! Faster!"

"Okay, man. You better hang on! Here we go!"

After taking him on a high speed lap around the hospital, we went back to the room to see if Heaven was done talking to the doctor. Our timing was perfect because Heaven was stepping into the hallway as we pulled up.

"You ready?" I asked.

"Yes. Let's get out of here so I can take my baby home."

We hopped in my Regal But instead of going to Heaven's house, I made a detour . "Why are you driving into Milwaukee?" She asked when she noticed that I was heading away from West Allis.

"I have to make a quick stop. I need to pick up something."

She gave me a look. "What are you picking up?"

"Just wait. You'll see."

I drove through Milwaukee's north side to the cemetery on Tetonia and Burleigh. When I pulled over and parked, Heaven frowned.

"What are we doing over here?"

"Look in the glove box and grab that envelope. I'll grab Mason."

"Wait! Robert, what are you doing?" Heaven called.

"Grab the envelope and come on," I told her as I opened the back door and picked up Mason.

She grabbed the envelope and climbed out of the car. "What are we doing at a cemetery."

"Do you trust me?"

She searched my eyes. "Yes."

"Come with me. I want to show you something."

I led the way through the graveyard with Heaven on the side of me.

"What is these?" Mason asked, pointing to the headstones.

"This is where people go before they go to heaven," I explained.

After walking about fifty yards, I stopped at a small white headstone. The name etched in the stone read Amelia Choeun. When Heaven seen it, her eyes grew wide and mouth dropped open. "How did you find her?"

"I started in city hall and went from there. It took a little bit of work, but I knew you needed to find her."

Heaven just stared at the grave. Then, she dropped to her knees and started sobbing. I put Mason down and squatted next to her, wrapping an arm around her shoulder.

"What's wrong, mommy? Why you sad?" Mason asked, wrapping his arms around her.

"I'm not sad, baby. I'm happy," she said, wiping her tears. Then, she turned to me.

"I don't even know what to say. I wasn't expecting this."

"You don't gotta say nothing. Open the envelope."

Her fingers shook as she opened the envelope and pulled out the single piece of paper. It was her mother's death certificate. "Oh my God, Robert! I am so speechless. I can't believe you did this. Thank you so much."

"You're welcome."

We sat at the gravesite for a few moments while Heaven mourned the loss of her mother and shed tears for finding her grave. When she was all cried out, we headed back to the car. She opened the door for me to put Mason in the backseat. After the little one was tucked away, I closed the door. When I turned, Heaven was waiting. She grabbed my shirt, lifting onto her tippy toes while pulling me in. Her lips were soft as cotton, her tongue slippery and sweet. It wasn't awkward like most first kisses. It was filled with the passion of lovers that had known each other's mouths for years. And when it ended, I wanted more.

"Thank you, Robert," she blushed, catching her breath. "For everything."

I just stared at her for a moment. Instead of talking, I bent down to kiss her again.

Chapter 19

Robert

The days began to fly by and before I knew it Thanksgiving had passed and Christmas was two weeks away. During the quick elapse of time, Heaven and I had become inseparable. I spent most of my time off work as well as my off days by her house. I was becoming addicted to her presence. Just having her in my life made me feel good. When I told my parents how our relationship had grown, they were ecstatic. Couldn't wait to meet her. I hadn't told my boys how I felt about her yet. But I would get around to it. One day.

"I know him," Heaven said, interrupting my thoughts.

We were at her house. She was sitting on my lap going through Facebook and Instagram profiles on her laptop. This was something like a ritual for her. She was determined to find the twins' father. And I was going to be right by her side all the way. Those boys needed that transplant and I would go through all kinds of hell along with Heaven until we found their father.

"You sure?" I asked, studying the picture.

His name was TL. He was light skinned with freckles. Wore his hair in matted dreadlocks and had a few gold teeth. This would be the third man I'd seen her contact.

"Yes. I don't know what I was thinking about with him. He looks like the Grinch that stole Christmas," she laughed.

"Yeah, you snapped with that one," I laughed. "Here. Get up. Let me use the bathroom," I said, wrapping my hands around her small waist and guiding her off my lap.

I had been in and out of the bathroom for the last hour messing with Ray. We played Call of Duty and the loser had to drink cups of water. I lost seven games in a row and now I was paying for it. When I came out of the bathroom, Heaven was feeling playful. She ran and jumped on me, making me fall on the couch.

"Whoa, girl! You about to kill me!"

She straddled my torso and pinned my arms down. "I want to look at you."

This was her thing. She would stare into my face for long periods of time without talking. At first I found it weird and creepy. After a few weeks, I got used to it. Now I liked it. It was very intimate. I had memorized her face and knew the most intimate details of her mug.

"Let's go somewhere," I said.

"Where? What about my kids?"

"Ray is fifteen. He got it. C'mon."

"But where are we going? It's getting late."

I looked at my watch. "It's only eight o'clock. And we're grown. It don't matter where we go. I just want to go there with you."

Emotions flashed in her eyes. "Okay. Let's go."

After telling Ray to watch the twins, we hopped in the Regal and I drove around aimlessly, talking and listening to old school love music. Al Green. Isley Brothers. Marvin Gaye. Luther Vandross. We were sitting at a stop light and I was serenading her along with Al Green when she perked up.

"Ooh! Let's go get some hot chocolate with candy canes!"

I turned to see what she was talking about. There was a mom and pop restaurant advertising hot cocoa with candy canes. We went inside and had drinks and watched the world outside through the big front window.

"Why did you go to jail, Robert? I've been trying to figure that out since you told me you did five years. You don't seem like the shoot em' up type, so what was it? Drugs?"

I could see excitement in her eyes as she awaited my response. My going to prison intrigued her. Problem was, I wasn't ready to talk about why I got locked up. It was complicated. Something I rarely talked about. Something I didn't want to be judged for. So I did what I said I wasn't going to do. Lied. "Yeah. Sold to an undercover," I said, breaking eye contact to look outside and take a sip from the mug of cocoa.

"So, how was it? Is prison like it is on Oz?"

I laughed. "Nah. Not in Wisconsin, at least. It's a mental thing. No raping, rioting, or killing. I mean, those things happen but it's rare. It's safer in prison than it is on the streets in Milwaukee. The hardest part about doing time is missing family and women. But I met some solid dudes that had my back and we helped each other get through the time. My boys Junior and Vito."

"Were they with you the night we met?"

"Yeah. Vito is a big dude with dreads and gold teeth. Junior was at the open mic. My other boy, Mike, was with us the night we met, too. He just caught a case and might get some time."

"Awe, that's messed up. I'm sorry to hear that. I hope they don't send him to jail. Tired of all my brothers ending up in prison."

"Amen to that. But enough about all this jail stuff. How about you let me listen to some of that poetry that God gifted you with the ability to write."

She turned red, looking nervously around the small eatery to see if anyone was in ear shot. "Right now?"

"Yeah. It's just me and you in this booth."

"Um..." She hesitated.

"Cmon, Heaven. You're good. Drop some of that heat, baby."

"Okay, okay. I wrote this a couple weeks ago. It's called You.

His eyes whispered to me across the room telling me what I've always wanted to hear.

When he came near, I felt my insides twitch.

When he spoke, the smooth baritones of his voice stuck to my ear drums like they were dipped in thick honey.

Not only was he beautiful and charming, but his aura was as majestic at the unicorns in my prepubescent dreams.

Songs by the R&B divas of my yesteryears play every time I'm in his presence. Whitney sings about the greatest love.

Miss Jackson makes me feel nasty.

Mariah whisks me away to a fairy tale love land.

And Aaliyah makes me want to tell him all of my secrets in a four page letter.

He told me how he feels about me is bigger than everything I've ever been through.

I've told him all the things about me that I've never been able to tell anyone else; because I trust...

You."

When Heaven finished reciting the poem, I gave a small ovation. "Wow! Whoever the dude is that inspired that sounds like he the truth!"

"You are so silly, Robert!" She blushed, pushing me playfully.

"I loved that poem, Heaven. For real. Best poem I ever heard."

"Thank you. You inspired it."

I acted surprised. "Really? I woulda never guessed that."

She shook her head. "Cocky and sarcastic. I wish you would've shown these qualities the night we met because I definitely wouldn't have talked to you."

"Yeah, right. You know you wanted to ride my wave, baby. I had that sauce dripping. Besides, according to the man code, we have to wait three months to show our flaws. I'm right on time."

"Man code? Seriously? You are way too much," she laughed.

"Man code is a real thing, baby. We got laws that govern our actions."

She shook her head. "Okay, Kevin Hart. How about we get out of here and get back to my munchkins."

"Cool, cool. I need to get some sleep anyway. We got a big order for tank parts at my job. I need eight hours so I can be on top of my game tomorrow."

We left the restaurant walking hand in hand. We were a few feet from my car when a raspy voice yelled from my left.

"Red Bone! Red Bone!"

I spun and seen a dark skinned man limping toward me with a cane. He was wearing a purple suit with a big white hat.

"I thought pimps were extinct," I cracked.

When I looked at Heaven, she wasn't laughing. She looked terrified. Like she seen a ghost.

"Red Bone! Red Bone! I know you hear me, girl!"

"What's up, Heaven? You good?"

"Can we just get in the car and leave? Please!"

I wanted to press her for more information but the look in her eyes told me everything I needed to know. Trouble was brewing. I popped the locks on the Regal and helped her into the car. I walked around to the driver's side but paused when the pimp spoke.

"Say, pat-na! Lemmie holla at chu!". His walk was cool but with purpose. His Shirley Temple curls bouncing with every step.

"What up, man?" I asked, studying his face.

He looked to be in his forties. Stood about 5'9". Slim build. Neatly trimmed facial hair. And his eyes were wide and glossy. I guessed he was high on coke because people that smoked weed didn't move that fast.

"Say, mane, my name is The Hoe Whisperer and I need to have a word with Red Bone," he said, looking past me and into the car.

I wanted to knock him out. He was disrespecting me by trying to talk to Heaven while she was with me. But I didn't feel like catching an assault charge on a pimp so I turned my back. "Move around, man. She don't want to talk to you," I said, opening the door to get in the car.

"Dig this, young playa. That there is mine and I want it back!" He yelled, grabbing the door to stop me from getting in the car.

I pushed him away. "Watch out, nigga. She don't wanna—"

I never got the chance to finish speaking. The Hoe Whisperer must've hit me because my lights went out.

Chapter 20

Heaven

I couldn't believe I had run onto The Hoe Whisperer again. My luck was terrible. I looked over when Robert grabbed the door handle. He was about to get in the car but Whisperer grabbed the door to stop him.

"Dig this, young playa! That there is mine and I want it back!"

"Watch out, nigga!" Robert yelled, shoving the pimp. "She don't wanna—"

Whisperer caught his balance and hit Robert with the cane. He went down, falling in between the door and driver's seat.

"Lil bitch ass nigga! I told you that hoe is mine. Let's go, Red Bone!"

I ignored Whisperer and scrambled across the seat to pull Robert in the car. I got him halfway in when he pushed me so hard that I tumbled in the passenger seat and landed against the door. When I looked up, Robert's fist was connecting with The Hoe Whisperer's chin. The pimp went out like a light. He collapsed in the middle of the street like all the bones had been snatched out of his body. The fight was obviously over but Robert jumped on top of him and began punching him in the face. If I didn't stop him he was going to kill Whisperer.

"No, Robert! Stop!"

I crawled across the driver's seat and stumbled out of the car. After I caught my balance, I jumped on Robert's back and tried to stop him. He shrugged me off easily, making me fall in the street before continuing to punish Whisperer's bloody face. I hurried from the ground and jumped on his back again. This time I wrapped my arms around his neck and legs around his waist.

"Robert, stop! Please!" I begged, shifting my weight and dragging him to the ground with me. I felt blood from his head wound on my face and tasted it in my mouth.

"Let me go, Heaven!" he yelled, trying to break my hold. I didn't let go.

"No. Stop. It's over."

"I said LET ME GO!" He roared and began standing to his feet while I was still hanging on his back.

Once I realized how easy he could handle my weight and that he wasn't attacking Whisperer again, I let him go.

"What the fuck is this, Heaven? What the fuck is this?" He yelled, oblivious to the blood pouring down his face from the head wound.

I was stuck. Didn't know what to say or how to explain who The Hoe Whisperer was.

"Say something, Heaven. I thought we told each other everything. I thought we put all of our secrets out there."

I left that part of my life out for a reason. I wanted to bury it. But now it had come back to life. I was trying to find the right words to explain this when I noticed crowds forming on both sides of the street. People had their phones out recording. Some of them were probably calling the police. I found my voice

"We have to go, Robert. Let's leave."

"We ain't going nowhere until you tell me who he is?"

I looked to the crowd again. They were chatting and pointing. "Robert, I think they're calling the police. We have to leave."

"Who is he, Heaven?"

I knew that he wasn't going to budge until I told him. So I lowered my head and whispered a response. "He was my pimp."

I expected Robert to start screaming his head off. But he started walking to the car. I chased him and was barely in the passenger seat when he sped away. He drove recklessly, not uttering a single word. Just mean mugged, shook his head, and breathed heavily. I don't ever remember being so scared. It was one thing when someone screamed when they got angry. At least you had some idea of what they would do. But Robert was quiet and that scared me more. I didn't know what he would do. I wasn't sure if I was going to die from a car accident or if he was going to flip out and kill me himself. All I could do was hold on and pray.

We had been driving for about five minutes when he brought the car to screeching stop in front of a liquor store. He got out and walked inside. I thought about leaving. I really wanted to drive away. But I didn't want to take his car and leave him stranded. I also felt like I owed him more than a nonverbal goodbye. So I sat and waited. He came out a few moments later guzzling a liter of Jack Daniel's. He looked like a crazy man with the liquor bottle and blood covering his face and clothes.

When he got back in the car, he continued to drive like a maniac while drinking from the bottle of whiskey like a thirsty man in a desert that found clean water. I had never seen him drink hard liquor, only beer. And that made me worry. Not about me, but him. I was worried that he didn't know what he was doing. He was losing control and the liquor was going to make it worse. I wanted to get out of the car, but couldn't. I didn't want to leave him alone. It took about twenty minutes for the liquor to kick in. He drank half the bottle and was having a hard time keeping the car straight.

"Pull over and let me drive, " I said.

"Nah, I got it, " he slurred, swerving a little.

Pictures of my children and little brother flashed in my head. "Robert, please pull over and let me drive."

He turned to face me, taking his eyes off the road to scream. "I said I got it!"

While he was yelling, the car began drifting into oncoming traffic. The bright lights of a big SUV flashed in our face.

"Robert, watch out!" I yelled, reaching for the steering wheel as my life flashed before my eyes. I grabbed the wheel just in time to yank us back into the flow of traffic.

"See what you almost made me do! Leave me alone and let me drive, nigga! " he yelled angrily. "I know what I'm doing. "

After the near death experience, I left him alone so he could focus all of his drunken attention on driving. I don't know how he did it, but he managed to get me home. When he stopped in the middle of the street in front of my house, I was so relieved.

"Get out," he slurred, staring at me through glossy red eyes.

I couldn't let him leave. Not in the condition he was in. "Robert, come in the house. You can't drive like this. "

"I said get out, nigga! Get out!" he yelled, barely able to keep his head from falling off his shoulders.

I reached over to grab his hand. "Robert, please. Come in the—"

"I SAID GET OUT! GET THE FUCK OUT! " he cursed and began banging his fists against the steering wheel. "GET THE FUCK OUT! "

I was so scared at the sudden and unexpected outburst that I didn't move. Tonight was the first time I'd ever heard him curse or seen him drunk and now he was spiraling out of control. Getting worse by the minute. For a moment, I thought he was about to attack me. Then, he stopped banging the steering wheel and became silent. Started looking out the windshield like someone was coming towards the car. When I followed his line of vision, I didn't see anybody. The streets were empty.

"Robert, what's going on?" I asked trying to get through the Jack Daniels.

He mumbled something that I couldn't understand.

"What did you say?"

"I killed Roger, " he mumbled.

Goosebumps spread across my skin and the hair on the back of my neck stood up. "What are you talking about?" I asked, making sure I heard him correctly.

Instead of answering me, he broke down crying. "I'm sorry, my nigga. I'm sorry, " he wept while continuing to stare out the windshield. "I'm sorry, brah."

I was so shocked and scared that all I could do was watch. He was unraveling and I didn't know what to do. Robert lowered his head onto the steering wheel and began sobbing like he was at a funeral. Real tears with real and gut wrenching emotions.

"Robert, what is going on?" I asked, reaching an arm around his shoulders while my other hand put the car in park and took the key from the ignition.

"It was an accident," he sobbed. "I didn't mean to do it. I'm sorry"

My heart and mind raced as I tried to put the pieces of the puzzle together to figure out what he was talking about and why he was crying. Roger was his brother. Did he really kill his own twin? I had to know.

"What did you do, Robert? What happened?"

He slid from the steering wheel and into my arms, his head on my bosom while continuing to cry. "I killed my brother, Roger. It was an accident. I'm sorry. It was an accident."

The confession stunned me, leaving my body numb. I didn't know how to respond. What could I possibly say? How could I comfort the pain of killing a sibling? He was hurting deep inside and the liquor had unleashed the scars on his soul. So I did the only thing I could. Held him and cried with him. When he was all cried out and blacked out, I pulled out my phone and called my little brother. I needed help getting Robert in the house.

"Where y'all at?" Ray answered.

"We in front of the house. Come outside. I need your help. Hurry up."

Ray came out of the house a few moments later and headed for the car. When he looked in the window, all he could see was Robert laid on top of me. "What's wrong? " he asked while snatching the door open.

" He's drunk. I need you to help me get him in the house."

Ray leaned in for a closer look. "Is that blood? What happened?"

"I don't got time to answer all the questions right now. We need to get him in the house."

"Okay," he agreed before grabbing Robert by the arm and lifting him up. "Robert, get up, man. I'ma help you in the house."

"Ray, that's you, lil nigga?" Robert slurred as he struggled to get out of the car.

"Yeah, this me. What happened, man?"

"I had to pull out these hands, my nigga," he laughed while holding onto my little brother. "I'm certified with these hands, boy!"

While Ray helped Robert towards the house, I went to park his car. We drug Robert to the bathroom where I stripped him naked and put him in the bath. I couldn't even enjoy washing him up because I was so worried about what the morning would bring. What would happen to us? How would he react when he remembered everything? Would he still want to be with me?

Chapter 21

Robert

My head felt like an entire drum line was inside my cranium banging away at their percussion instruments. I let out a moan while reaching for my hurting head. And that's when I felt the bandage. My eyes shot open but the light made me close them again. My world began spinning and the banging in my head became louder. It took a few moments for the pain to go away and I was finally able to open my eyes again. That's when I noticed I was in Heaven's bed. I tried to remember how the hell I got in her bed but I drew a blank.

"Good morning," Heaven said.

"How did I get in your bed?" I asked, my throat dry like I had drank desert sand.

She gave a worried look. "You don't remember?"

I stared into those beautiful eyes for a moment and was transported back to last night. The memories rushed into my brain, making my head hurt even worse. The pimp hit me with the cane. I beat him up and then went to get something to drink. The rest was blank. I closed my eyes as the weight of it all dawned on me. She used to be a prostitute. Sold her body for profit. She even had a pimp. What the hell was I going to do? I was feeling her on every level, but that was before I knew she used to be a whore. Movement from Heaven made me open them again. She was sitting up, back against the headboard, watching me. Waiting. I took my time, searching for to right words.

"Is it true? " I mumbled.

She looked away for a moment, the shame washing over her beautiful face. Then, she looked me in my eyes and nodded. "Yes. It's true."

148

Even though I already knew that the man was her pimp, hearing her confirm it felt like I got hit in the head with the cane all over again. My temples throbbed like they were about to burst. I reached for my head again to massage the pain.

"There are Tylenol's and water next to you," she said.

I looked on the bedside table and seen the pills and a bottle of water. I was reaching for the medicine when I felt that I was naked. I looked under the covers to confirm my suspicion and then at Heaven.

"Did we..."

"No. I had to wash you up. Your clothes are right there. " She pointed to the folded clothes on the dresser.

I took the pills and quenched my thirst with the bottle of water, all the while asking myself if I really wanted to know the truth. Could I handle it? What would I do once I found out? I wasn't sure. But I had to know.

"Why didn't you tell me you used to be a prostitute?"

She let out a stressed breath. "I was embarrassed, Robert. I didn't know how to say it. I care about what you think about me. I didn't want you to change your opinion. The way you look at me makes me feel like the most beautiful woman in the world. Nobody has ever made me feel that way before and I didn't want that to change."

Her words sounded sincere but I was no longer sure that I could trust her. "In the hospital, I thought we told each other everything. How could you keep something this serious from me? What if he would've killed me? "

"I'm sorry, Robert. I know I should've told you but I was scared. I never wanted to put you through this. "

We were silent for a moment. I needed to know more. "How did you get a pimp, Heaven? How did you get into that life? What am I supposed to think now?"

She looked towards the window and let out a deep breath. When she looked at me again, the truth began to flow like a river. "After I ran away from home, I tried living on the streets but I didn't know what I was doing. I slept in an abandoned house the first night and was scared out of my mind. I didn't want to spend another night in the abandoned house so I told myself that I would have to figure something out. The next day, I was walking down the street and met a boy named Boosie. He asked me if I wanted to kick it with him. I was broke with nowhere to go so I agreed. He ended up being a drug dealer and I rode around with him while he sold drugs. I met some of his friends and they became my friends. I started sleeping with all of them for money, drugs, and a place to sleep. I did this for a couple of months before KB's baby mama caught us together and beat me up. I ran out of the house half naked and into a woman named April. And that's when my life changed.

"April was beautiful. She wore expensive clothes and drove a pink Benz. She gave me some clothes and offered me a ride. I told that her I didn't have anywhere to go and that I was basically homeless. She said she would help me. She convinced me that me and her were just alike. She told me that she ran away from home at a young age, how she was once homeless, and that she was able to get off the streets. Then, she took me to a house she shared with five other women and they told me they would be my new family. All of the girls embraced me like a little sister and told me about the life. They made it sound glamorous. Money, cars, jewelry, trips, and fancy clothes. I was a teenager so I accepted their explanation and wanted to be like them. They cleaned me up, gave me a makeover, and introduced me to Whisper when he came home later that night."

"Whisper made me feel like I could do anything. He talked to me like I was a grown up and promised that if I stuck with him, I would never go broke or hungry. He promised that he would give me the world and that I would be famous like a movie star. And I believed him. When he took me to turn my first trick, I was scared as hell but I did it because I wanted to please him and my sisters. I wanted to fit in with the family. We went to an expensive hotel where I met a white man dressed in a suit. I was inexperienced and young, and he liked it. After it was over, I went back to Whisper and he told me how good I did and that he was proud of me. I actually felt like I really did something good. When I went back to the girls, they encouraged me the same way that Whisper had. Told me I did a good job and I was their sister. And that's how we lived for three years.

"The problems started when I fell in love with Whisper. I had never been in a real relationship or had a father growing up so I didn't know how love was supposed to go. All I knew is that Whisper told me he loved me and took care of me. I thought that was love. I fantasized having his kids and settling down. When I told April, she told me I was tripping. She told me that Whisper didn't really love me, he loved his money. So I got the thought that if I brought more money, that he would drop the other girls and be with me. That if I earned enough, he would only want me. But it didn't work out like that. The more money I got, the more he wanted. When I saw that my plan wasn't working, I gave him an ultimatum. I told him that I wanted to be his woman and that if he didn't let the other girls go and be with me, I was leaving. Instead of agreeing, he laughed at me and told me I would always belong to him and to go get his money.

" I was crushed that my plan didn't work and went to my room and packed my bags. I was about to leave out the front door when Whisper attacked me. I fought him back and that made him beat me worse. My face was busted and bleeding and I think my ribs were broken. When he put me in the car, I thought he was taking me to the hospital but instead he dropped me off on 35th and Lisbon and told me to get his money. That's when I realized that he didn't love me and I swore that I was never going back to him. I knew a girl that lived in the area and she let me stay with her until I was well enough to move around. Her brother liked me so I started messing around with him so I could have somewhere to live. When I was fully healed, I went back to the street and started turning tricks again. I felt free to do whatever I wanted to do. I was grown with no responsibilities and nobody watching over me or telling me what to do. I ran the streets and partied and stayed high so I wouldn't have to think about what I was doing. One day, I woke up sick and started throwing up. At first I thought I was sick because of drugs. I used Percs and Heroin and when I didn't have any, I got sick. But the drugs didn't stop me from waking up sick. That's when my friend told me that I might be pregnant. I didn't believe her but I still went and got a test. Sure enough, I was pregnant. I wasn't about to raise a baby so I went to get an abortion and ran into Reesy. She helped me change my life and become the person I am today. I hadn't seen Whisper since I left his house all those years ago until a couple of months ago while I was trying to get someone's DNA. He tried to get me back but Ron stood up for me. Whisper promised that he would get me and that's what happened last night."

I didn't know what to say. The only thing that I could think was that she had really been a prostitute. She already told me she didn't know how many people she slept with and now I knew why.

"I don't even know what to say, Heaven," I confessed. " I wish you would've told me all of this while we were in the hospital. I feel like you hid that part of your life from me on purpose, hoping that I would never find out and now I got a busted up forehead and don't know what to think. Is that it? Is there anything else that you're not telling me?"

"That's it, Robert. I swear on my life I don't have any more secrets. That's everything."

I was quiet again, thinking. Would we be able to be out in public and not run into people that she had been with?

How many people had we passed in the streets that knew who she was? What would my parents think? What would my boys think?

"You don't have anything to say?" She asked, searching my face.

I didn't want to tell her what I was thinking so I climbed out of bed and went for my clothes. "I need some time to think."

I kept my back to her as I got dressed but I could hear her crying. A part of me wanted to get back in bed and console her. She was a kid when she got involved in prostitution and probably thought she didn't have many options. However, another part of me was angry from all the deceit and wanted to get away. So I ignored her tears while sliding into my shoes.

"I thought you said how you feel about me is bigger than everything that I've been through."

Her words grabbed my attention, forcing me to look at her. I saw the pain in her eyes and the shame on her face. She bared her soul and I had judged her. She knew my opinion of her had changed. And there was nothing that I could do about it.

"All of this is a lot, Heaven. I just need some time. I'll call you later. "

Chapter 22

Heaven

"I hate men. If I didn't love God so much, I would become a lesbian," I vented in frustration as I drove down Sherman Boulevard.

"Oh, Heaven! Don't go there, baby girl," Reesy laughed. "You gave him a lot to think about. It may take a little time."

"It's been two days! He said he was going to call me later that night. That was two days ago!"

"Worrying about it won't change anything. Did you try to call him?"

I thought about how many times I picked up the phone and let my finger hover over his name. "No, I didn't. He said he would call me. I don't want to seem like I'm desperate. I wanted to respect his space. He said he needed time to think."

"Heaven, in this day and age, women go after what we want. It's not desperate to be assertive. When men go after what they want, that's called being a go getter. Why can't that apply to women as well? If you want answers to your questions, I think you should call him. Don't wait around being passive and wait for him to make the first move. Faith without action is dead. You have to pray about it and then go and do your part. Don't just sit around and wait for God to drop something in your lap. Sometimes you have to go out and get what God is giving you."

Reesy's words caused me to pause and think. "But what if he doesn't want to be with me anymore? "

"But what if had does?"

"I don't know, Reesy. I think I'm scared of being rejected."

"Well, you better get over your fears. We are more than conquerors through Christ Jesus."

I needed to know how he felt. I needed answers. "Okay. I'm going to call him as soon as I'm done with this run."

"Good. Where are you going?"

"I'm meeting with a guy named Durk. More paternity tests."

"Okay. I'll be praying for you, baby girl. You got this."

"Thanks. Bye."

After ending the call with Reesy, I thought about Robert some more as I drove. I was in love with him. Real, I will make a fool of myself for him, love. I needed him. I didn't want to go another moment without talking to him. Two days without his presence was killing me. So as soon as I got this DNA sample from Durk, I was going to track him down and make him face me. I needed answers. I turned onto 36th and Custer a few moments later and looked for a green Audi truck on chrome wheels. It wasn't hard to find. When I pulled behind it, a heavy set brown skinned man with red dyed dreadlocks climbed from the passenger seat and walked towards my passenger door. I searched his face for similarities to my kids as he opened the door. There was no resemblance.

"What's good, shorty?" he grinned, smelling like weed and chicken as he climbed in. "Been a minute, huh?"

I broke out the tube and handed him the swab. "It has. I just need you to swab your cheek a couple of times."

"All business, huh?" he asked, taking the swab.

"I don't mean to be rude but I've just been going through something."

"I understand." He nodded. "Life be hard sometimes. This is some official, shit, right? You ain't finna fuck with a nigga DNA on no bullshit, right?"

I showed him the case I was going to put the swab in. "It's official. I need to know who my twins father is and I don't want my business all over social media or in the courts."

"Fa sho." He nodded. "I definitely don't wanna be in no courtrooms," he said before sticking the swab in his mouth and handing it back to me. "How long before I'ma know something?"

" The only way you're going to hear from me again is if you're the father. Takes about ten days."

"You say they twins, huh?"

I nodded while going through my phone to show him a picture. "Beautiful twin boys."

"Yeah, they cute. Let me know something, shorty," he said while reaching for the door.

"Thanks. I will."

After Durk got out of the car, I drove away thinking about what I was going to say to Robert. I wanted to know how he felt about me but I wasn't sure if that was the first question I should ask. *'Hey. How are you doing? How do you feel about me?'* didn't sound right. After going back and forth about what to say, I made the call. My heart raced in my chest as the phone rang. After about five rings, it went to voicemail. I thought about calling again but I didn't want to seem like a crazy person. He probably didn't answer for a reason. I was about to check his Facebook to see if he was online when my phone started ringing. It was a number I didn't recognize.

"Hello?" I answered.

"You have a call from an inmate in the Milwaukee county jail," a robotic voice began speaking.

I was wondering who was calling me from jail when I heard his voice.

"This is Robert, " he said before the robot voice started giving more instructions.

I listened intently as the robot began giving instructions all the while wondering why in the hell Robert was in jail.

"To accept the call, press 5."

I pressed five as fast as my finger could move.

"You may now begin to speak. Thank you for using Century Link."

"Hello!? Robert?"

"Hey, Heaven. We don't have that much time to talk. This is a quick call so the voice system can tell you how to put money on the phone. I need to talk to you. I've missed you."

Hearing him say those words made my heart skip a beat. "I missed you too. Why are you in jail?"

"The police were waiting at my house when I went home. They arrested me for beating up Whisper. I had to spend the weekend in jail because there are no bail hearings on the weekend. We'll talk more about it when I call back. The voice is about to explain how to set up an account. Do you have a credit card with you?"

"Yes. I'm pulling over right now. How soon can you call again?"

"I'm calling back in ten—"

"Thank you for using Century Link," the robot voice cut in. "To create an account, press 1."

I pulled to the side of the road and followed the instructions to open a prepaid account. When it was done, I watched the clock on my phone, counting the minutes until Robert would call back. When I replayed him saying that he missed me, my insides began bubbling and I felt naturally high. The smile on my face was so wide that I could see all of my teeth when I looked in the rearview mirror. Then finally, ten minutes later, he called.

"Robert?"

"It sounds so good to hear your voice."

"Awe!" I gushed, almost bursting into tears. "It sounds good to hear your voice, too. I thought you didn't want to talk to me anymore."

"It wasn't like that, Heaven. I just needed some time to think. The last thing I was expecting was to go home and get arrested, but it did me some good to get away from everybody and everything and get my mind together. Being in a room by yourself can be therapeutic. There are no distractions and you can really put things into perspective. I'm sorry that it took me so long to call but I needed to be sure that I was making the right decision."

Hearing the part about the *'right decision'* made me a little nervous. I held myself in check, hoping my voice didn't crack when I spoke.

"So, what did you decide?" I asked, wincing a little while hoping for the best and expecting this worst.

"I decided that how I feel about you is bigger than everything that you've been through. I don't want to live without you. I really need you in my life, Heaven. I need you like the air I breathe and I will kick ten pimps ass if they try to come in between us."

I bust out laughing as happy tears spilled down my face. "Awe, Robert, I need you, too. And I don't know if this is too early to say this, but I need you to know how I feel. I love you, Robert."

There was a pause on his end. "You know what's crazy?" he chuckled.

"What?"

"All day I've been trying to figure out how to tell you the same thing. I'm in love with you too, Heaven."

That was it. At that moment I could've died and went to heaven. I felt so good. I was higher than I had been during all the days of my drug use. "It feels so good to hear you say that, Robert. I need to see you. Can I come see you or bail you out?"

"That's already been taken care of. My boys paid my bail already and are outside waiting for me to get processed out."

I felt a little sad that I couldn't go get him. "Okay. So, how long until you get out?"

"I don't know. I've been waiting for about an hour already. I planned on telling you all of this in person but they were taking too long to let me go so I decided to call."

"I'm glad you called because I don't think I could've gone another moment without hearing from you. I just called your phone and was about to stalk your Facebook."

"I knew you had some crazy stalker in you. Pretty people always got them Halle Berry issues," he cracked.

"Forget you, Robert! " I laughed. "You're the one in jail calling me crazy. How does that work?"

After we shared another laugh, I got serious. A question popped into my head that demanded answering.

"Robert, do you really think you can handle everything that I've been through? I know that it can't be easy for a man to be with someone with a past like mine. There is no telling when someone or something from my past might pop up again and I want to know if you will be able to handle it with me. I really love you and care about you and I don't want us to fall apart because of something that neither one of us can control."

"I'm not going to lie, Heaven. I thought about that a lot. Not knowing who you slept with or how many people you slept with was messing with me. The thought of walking by strangers and not knowing if they were a part of your past is not going to be easy. Neither is the thought of us having more encounters with pimps or anybody else that has been with you or wants to be with you. But I also know that nothing worth having is easily gained. If you really want something, you have to work for it. I'm ready to put in the work, Heaven.

You are my world. I love you. I'm ready. Together, we can handle anything."

More tears spilled down my face. "Oh, Robert! I love you, too. You have me sitting here crying my eyes out like a baby."

"As long as they are happy tears, it's all good."

"Yes, they are happy tears. I've never been happier in my life."

I sat on the side of the road and talked to Robert for forty five minutes before they finally released him. He told me to go home and that he would come over after he went home to freshen up. But I couldn't wait another moment to be with him. I didn't want to wait for him to come over. I was going to him.

Chapter 23

Robert

Man it felt good to be free!

I stepped out of the Milwaukee County Jail feeling like I had been freed from doing hard time in prison. That's what a weekend of sleeping on the floor and eating soggy bologna sandwiches would do to you. Make two days feel like a year. After taking in the sights and sounds of being free in downtown Milwaukee, I searched for my boys and spotted Vito's Lexus. I began walking towards the car when Mike climbed from the passenger seat.

"So this is what fighting with pimps and spending the weekend in jail looks like, huh?" He grinned, ribbing my shabby appearance.

My sweater and pants were blood stained and I had a scar on my forehead from the cane.

"It never stops, huh? See it say it, right?"

"I wouldn't be me if I didn't call it how I see it, " he smiled while opening his arms for a hug. "But I'm glad that you out. And damn you need to take a shower, nigga. Whooweee, you stank!" he laughed while fanning his nose.

"Forget you, dog. For real. You ain't on nothing," I laughed while climbing in the backseat next to Junior

"Welcome back to freedom, " Jr. said as we shook hands.

"Yeah, Welcome back to this side. And Mike is right. You do need a shower," Vito laughed.

"Man, forget all of y'all. I just spent two days sleeping on the floor and eating bologna sandwiches and this what I gotta get out to? I wasn't in a hotel. I was in jail."

"And you smell like it," Junior added, pinching his nose.

"How you go to jail for fighting a pimp anyway? " Vito laughed again. "I thought them niggas was extinct."

"So did I. But this dude had the suit, the perm, and wore gators."

"You mean to tell me that you let a nigga with alligator shoes on and wearing a perm do that to your head? " Mike asked, pointing to my wound as Vito drove away.

"He came from behind me. I was getting in the car and didn't see him."

"I thought I taught you better than that. You never take your eyes off the enemy, fool."

"Man, this ain't nothing compared to what I did to him, " I said, trying to save face. "You see I'm the one that went to jail. I punished him."

"You better had, nigga. Cause ain't no way you about to be kicking it with me and you let a pimp serve you."

"Whatever, man." I waved him off. "If you wanna see me in action, let me know. I'll put hands on you too."

"Talk to 'em then, Robert! " Vito cheered, trying to geek us up.

"Man, ain't no R&B singer finna do nothing to me," Mike laughed.

"What's up with Heaven, though? She really had a pimp?" Junior asked. "She don't seem like the type."

"They never do," Mike cut in. "It always be the ones you least expect."

"Man, you don't even know what you talking about, brah," I defended. "She got involved in that after she ran away from home as a teenager. She didn't know any better."

"That's part of pimping," Vito said. " You know that's how they like to do. Catch 'em while they young and don't know no better. They easier to break in than an older female."

"Okay, pimping! I didn't know you had it in you, Vito," Junior laughed.

"I was sipping pimp juice way before Nelly made the song," Vito cracked, popping his collar.

"It don't matter how old she was when she got turned out, my nigga," Mike cut in. "She was a night stalker. Get paid to play type of broad. Once you in, you in for life. That's law, my nigga!"

I shook my head. "Not her. She a different woman. She gave her life to God and she's celibate."

Mike spun in the seat to face me, a challenge in his eyes. "She celibate like you, huh?"

The look in his eyes told me that he knew something. I just didn't know what. So I kept up the lie. "Yeah. She's celibate like me. "

Mike erupted with laughter like he was watching TikTok videos.

"C'mon, man," Junior groaned, shaking his head.

I looked back and forth from Mike to Junior They knew something. My body began to grow warm as I realized my secret had been uncovered.

"What's funny, Mike? Why he laughing, Jr? " I asked.

Junior turned his head to look out the window. "I don't know what that nigga on."

I turned back to Mike and waited for him to stop laughing. When done, he looked at me, amusement dancing in his eyes while he spoke calmly. "We know you ain't celibate, brah. We been knew. We was waiting on you to keep it real with us."

I looked from Mike to Junior and Vito. Neither one of them would look me in my eyes. I felt like the biggest fakest fraud in the world. When I turned back to Mike, he was smiling like a detective that had cracked a tough case. All I could do was shake my head and laugh.

"Man, why you didn't say something a long time ago? How you gon' let me walk around all this time lying?"

"Because you wanted to. I can't stop nobody from doing what they wanna do. So, we let you."

"Junior and Vito, one of y'all could've said something. I expect Mike to do something like that but not y'all."

"It was yo lie, brah. We let you tell it," Vito said.

"I wanted to say something but I didn't think it was my place," Junior said. "It was something that you was going through, you know? So we let you have it."

I shook my head again. "How y'all find out?"

Mike still had the amused look in his eyes when he spoke. "Heard it from the horse's mouth. "

"Sapphire?" I asked.

He nodded. "The horse with the really talented mouth."

I stared him in his eyes for a moment trying to see if he was saying what it sounded like he was saying. He stared back at me, confirming my suspicions.

"You fucked Sapphire! " I blurted.

He shrugged his shoulders nonchalantly. "Who didn't?"

It felt like I had been punched in my chest by a burning fist. My body grew hot as anger and betrayal surged through me. "You fucked Sapphire? " I asked again, ready to punch Mike in the mouth.

"You mad?" He frowned, leaning back a little.

"Am I mad? Hell yeah, I'm mad, nigga! How you gon' sleep with my ex?"

Mike brushed off my anger. "You really in yo' chest about a certified thot, brah? We really about to get into over Sapphire?"

"It ain't about Sapphire, nigga. It's the principle. You know you can't sleep with none of our exes. You crossed the line."

"I ain't the only one that crossed the line," he said, looking at Junior

"C'mon, Mike! Why you put me in this shit, nigga? " Junior snapped.

I couldn't believe what I was hearing. "You too?"

He reached for my hand, sorrow in his eyes. "Brah, it wasn't like that. One thing led to another and the next thing you know…"

I slapped his hand away and turned to Vito. "You too, Vito?"

"Nah, brah. This the first time I'm hearing about this right now. I don't smash the homies thotties."

I turned to mug Mike one more time before looking out the window. I couldn't believe my boys had sex with my ex.

"C'mon, Rob. You know she wasn't shit. We did you a favor, nigga," Mike said.

"Leave me alone right now. I ain't got no holla," I said, focusing my attention on the passing scenery so I wouldn't fight my boys.

"Mike might be right, brah," Vito cut in. "Sapphire ain't shit, man. Now you know."

"Man, that nigga been knew that shit all the way back in high school," Mike said. "She fucked the whole basketball team and broke bad on you when you got locked up. Plus, she lied to him about being her baby daddy. She a hoe and she been a hoe. You can't be mad at yo' niggas for treating a hoe like a hoe. We ain't the ones tripping. You is."

I kept staring out the window trying to make sense of my thoughts and feelings. A part of me admitted that Mike had a point. Sapphire had done me bogus time and time again. And she was also a Hoe with a capital H. But I still felt something for her and I didn't want my boys having sex with her.

"Look at me, Rob," Mike said.

I kept looking out the window.

"We been niggas for most of our life and this how it's finna be? We finna fall out over the biggest hoe of all hoes?" He asked.

I turned to look at him, the anger still blazing through my body and in my eyes. "You always gon' be my nigga, but you bogus. And you too, Junior"

"My bad, Rob. For real. I wasn't try'na go there but she came on to me," Jr. said somberly.

"I ain't sorry," Mike said. "You needed to feel this so you can stop trusting these hoes. They ain't loyal. Sapphire never been loyal. The first time Jr. hit her, she blessed us both at the same time. Let yo' niggas run a train. C'mon, my nigga. What is that?"

I was surprised to hear they had a threesome. "Y'all ran a train?"

"She wanted it, brah," Jr. shrugged.

"One in the front and one in the back. A hoe, my nigga," Mike added.

I shook my head and went back to staring out the window. How could I be mad at my boys for treating a freak like a freak. Being mad at them was a waste of energy. Sapphire wasn't worth any more of my thoughts or energy.

"Y'all still should've told me," I sulked.

"Yeah, you right about that. I should've said something. I should've been let you know that she got down," Mike said. "But ain't no sense in crying over spilled milk."

"So, is we still niggas? " Jr. asked, putting a hand on my shoulder. "It only happened one time and I won't ever do nothing like that again. On my life."

I cracked a smile as we shook hands. "We good, brah. We locked in for life."

"Shake my hand too, nigga," Mike said, grabbing my hand. "We still niggas, right?"

"Man, you know you still my boy no matter how much you piss me off."

"Tough love is real love, my nigga. And believe me when I tell you that Heaven is from the same tree as Sapphire. They tainted fruit, brah. They hoes."

I could feel my anger starting to rise again. "C'mon, Mike. You don't even know her. I keep telling you she ain't like that. And she definitely ain't nothing like Sapphire."

"What do you mean? She used to sell pussy. How come she ain't a hoe?"

"Because she changed and I believe her. She not what you think she is. We all changed and grew up. She did the same thing."

"You just a sucka for love, nigga. Heaven is still a hoe, brah. You need to wise up and fall back or share her with the homies," he laughed.

"Call her another hoe and we boxing!" I snapped. My anger had boiled over and I was about to knock my boy out.

"Hold on, y'all. Chill!" Jr. said, ready to jump in between us.

Mike looked like I had just told him that someone died. Pain spread across his face and his mouth hung open in disbelief. "You gon' fight me over a female, brah? For real?"

"I told you to stop calling her out of her name. She ain't like that. She a good woman. Sapphire was a hoe. I can't defend that. But Heaven is different."

Mike still wore the look of disbelief. "You wanna fight me over a female, brah? For real?"

"I want you to stop calling my girl out of her name."

"Yo' girl?" Mike asked, spinning around and flopping down in the seat. "Take me to get some weed, Vito. I need to smoke something. This nigga is tripping."

"It's gon' be aight," Vito laughed. "People grow up and change. We gotta give her a chance. She might be good for him."

Mike mugged Vito. "What is you talking about? She used to have a pimp. Listen to what you saying."

"You in love, huh?" Jr. asked.

I nodded. "Yeah, brah. I think she is the one."

Junior smiled. "I'm happy for you, man. You a grown man and can make your own decisions. I think you know what you doing. If she's the one, I support you."

"So do I," Vito added. "Everybody deserve a second chance. Never know who God got for you until you find them."

Mike shook his head. "Why is you niggas encouraging this bullshit? Hurry up and take me to get some gas so I can get lifted. You niggas is really blowing me."

I put a hand on my boy's shoulder. "I know what I'm doing, Mike. I appreciate the concern, but I got it."

He shrugged my hand from his shoulder. "Don't touch me, nigga. You might infect me with the sucka virus and have me fall in love with Sapphire."

All I could do was laugh. When Vito turned onto my block, I immediately noticed Heaven's car parked in front of my house. My heart started beating faster in anticipation of seeing my woman.

"Who car is that? " Vito asked as he slowed down.

"That's Heaven," I answered proudly, opening the door before he could stop the car. "Stop right here and let me out."

I was already halfway out of the car before he was able to park. I took long strides towards her car . When the driver's door opened, she came running towards me.

Chapter 24

Heaven

I sat in my car in front of Robert's house anxiously awaiting his arrival. After I got off the phone with him, there was so much more that I wanted to say and so much more that I wanted to know. I wanted to tell him that I loved him until I couldn't talk anymore and I wanted to hear him repeat it to me until his lips fell off. But more than anything, I wanted to touch him. I wanted to feel his strength and smell his scent. I wanted him more than I had ever wanted anything in my life. And just when I thought that I couldn't stand waiting any longer, I watched through my rearview mirror as a yellow Lexus turned onto the block and began slowing down. Without even seeing him, I knew Robert was in that car. I could feel it. When the rear passenger door opened and he jumped out, I ran to meet him.

Time seemed to slow down as we moved towards one another. He still wore the same blood stained clothes that he left my house wearing two days ago but he still looked good. By far, the most handsome man on the entire planet. And now he was all mine. When I was close enough, I launched myself at him, knowing that he would catch me. He caught me like men catch women in the movies. I wrapped my arms around his neck, legs around his waist, and attacked his face with an *'I love you and I miss you kiss'*. His lips were warm and soft, his tongue juicy and wet. I probed his mouth as our tongues did an erotic dance. I don't know how long the kiss lasted, but I never wanted it to stop. Unfortunately, we both needed a break to catch our breath.

"Hey, you," he smiled, giving me another peck on the lips.

"Hey, to you too," I said, staring lovingly into his beautiful eyes.

"I told you I was coming over."

"I couldn't wait that long. I need you now."

I could see the question light his eyes. He wondered if I was saying what it sounded like I was saying.

"Yo, Robert! We about to hit it. Get at me later, " one of his friends called.

"Okay. Later," he called over his shoulder, never taking his eyes off me. "You sure about this?"

I was done talking so I responded with a kiss. We continued the passionate lip lock as he carried me towards his house and up the stairs. When we were standing at the door, we stopped kissing so he could dig the keys out of his pocket. I thought about climbing down off of him but I didn't want to let him go. I felt connected to him in every possible way: spiritually, emotionally, mentally, and sexually. If I let him go now, it might ruin the connection. So I held on and found his lips again, keeping our bodies connected for as long as I could.

My feelings in that moment told me that I had found what I was looking for. Robert was the reason I had become celibate. We had taken away the physical aspect of our relationship until love blossomed. This was the way God intended. And I was being rewarded with feelings that I had never felt before or knew existed. All I knew was that whatever happened behind this door would be life changing.

When he finally got the keys from his pocket and opened the door, we twisted, turned, grinded, and danced until I was in my panties and bra, he in his boxers, standing outside his bedroom door. We stood facing one another, drinking in the sight of our almost nude bodies. Goosebumps popped up all over my skin, my nipples got hard, and the girl below my waist was dripping wet. I had seen his body twice and knew his intimate parts from giving him a bath a few days ago. But I still drank him in with my eyes like I was seeing him for the first time. His body was tight and defined.

Lean muscle. If I had ever pictured the body of a real man in my head, it belonged to him. His skin was a deep and rich brown. His scars were in all their right places. His face was strong but soft. His eyes smoldering. The veins in his neck threatened to burst from the blood rushing. The bulge in his boxers leaving no mistake that he was ready, willing, and more than capable. I could feel the sexual energy emanating from him like radiation from a nuclear reactor. Once our energies combined and collided, we would be complete.

"You ready?" He asked, being the gentleman that he was.

Anticipation had me speechless. I closed my eyes and nodded. He reached down and lifted me in his strong arms, carrying me across the threshold like a husband does his wife. I felt special. Loved. Wanted. Desired. I wrapped my arms around his neck, finding his lips again as he carried me to the bed. He lay me down gently and stood over me, taking in the sight of my body. Like he was trying to etch all of me into his memory. I wasn't an insecure woman, but being under his stare was a little intimidating. Then, he reached down and undid my bra clasp. My breasts popped out like freed slaves. He kneeled on the bed, lowering his head until I felt his mouth on my nipple.

"Oooh!" I moaned.

I cannot ever remember feeling so much pleasure from someone's mouth on my breast. Electricity traveled up and down my body like a live current. Then, he moved his lips to my other nipple and made me feel everything all over again. After making love to my breasts with his mouth, he stood and removed his boxers. His manhood stood at attention. I couldn't take my eyes off of it. It was long, thick, straight, and beautiful. He knelt next to me and pulled off my panties then climbed between my legs. I trembled when our skin touched. I could feel his heat. His energy. His need. He lowered his mouth to mine as his penis found my other lips. When he entered me, I felt the stiffest, hardest, fullest, and most welcomed flesh that I had ever known. And to my surprise, it didn't hurt. If felt good. Like he belonged inside of me. My body surrendered as he took control.

For the first time in my life, I felt secure and loved. My body erupted with pleasure. He stroked me long and deep. He was strong and gentle. And then I had another first. For the first time in my life, I had an orgasm from intercourse. It was intense! Like everything inside of me had dissolved into a million pieces and traveled down to my vagina. I dug my nails into his shoulders and back while my body jerked and spasmed. I screamed and spoke in different tongues. I felt tears spill from my eyes and down my face. I was complete. Robert continued to love me steadily, his hands locking fist fulls of my hair and tugging just enough. I loved it! When he began to speed up, I knew he was reaching his peak. I held on as he dug into me faster and harder. The muscles in his body began to constrict and tighten as he went faster. And then he exploded. A grunt came from somewhere deep inside him as his stick spasmed, coating my insides with his juices. He fell on top of me and we lay there, listening to each other's breathing. I could feel our hearts merge and begin to beat as one. My body was locked so tightly into his that no part was unfamiliar.

Then, I got a sudden urge to have more of him. He had awakened something deep inside of me and I felt more alive than I've ever felt. I wanted more of him. All of him. So I flipped him onto his back, making sure to keep him snugly inside me. My body was starved and hungry. Robert was the main course. I lowered my head to nibble a spot on his neck, stopping to lick and suck like there was chocolate there. The left side, right side, his throat. He moaned approvingly, his hands locking onto my waist. I rocked my hips back and forth and could feel him slowly coming back to life inside of me. When he was fully awake, I sat upright and closed my eyes, clearing my mind of everything except his body and mine. I rode hard and fast, losing myself in the passion. I called his name as I pushed down onto him and he thrust up into me. I was rapidly climbing the mountain of pleasure. When I got to the top, my mind went blank.

"Oh God!" I screamed as another orgasm took hold of my body.

His big hands clamped down on my waist and hips as he erupted inside me again. That sent me over the edge. The second orgasm better than the first. I could feel it vibrating through my body in waves of pleasure as I fell on top of him. I was exhausted. Drained. Satisfied. And in love.

Chapter 25

Robert

If climbing Mount Everest or flying into outer space made a man feel like he accomplished the greatest feat that the world had ever known, then those men must've never been in love. Not puppy love but deep, passionate, self-sacrificing, life changing love. The kind of love that made you want to stay in the house instead of going out with the fellas. Made you want to forget every past lover because there was no comparing. Made it so no material possession mattered: money, cars, clothes, jewelry. At this moment, I would have traded it all.

Heaven was sleeping peacefully on my chest, her breathing light, body warm. She fit perfectly against me. Like her body was made for mine. And as I lay in bed thinking about how perfect she was for me, I thought about what today was. Christmas. The day that I was taking Heaven to meet my parents. I was excited about the holiday meal and meeting. I wanted my parents to see that I had met a good woman. And deep down inside, I wanted my father to approve of her the most. Even though I was almost thirty years old, having his approval still meant the world to me.

The pitter patter of feet disturbed my morning reflections. It was the twins. They were running towards Heaven's door with a purpose. Without warning, they burst into the room. "Mommy, mommy! Santa Claus came last night and he left a whole bunch of presents!" Mason screamed, his eyes wide with excitement. "Get up, mommy! Get up!" He yelled, jumping in bed and tugging on her arm.

"Wait, y'all. Wait!" Heaven said groggily, trying to gather herself.

"C'mon, Robert! Come and see what Santa Claus gave us," Jason yelled at me, pulling my arm.

Me and Heaven were naked beneath the covers and needed a moment to get dressed. So I threw the boys a challenge. "Meet me in the living room. Last one to the tree is a rotten egg!"

As soon as the words left my lips, the twins took off running as fast as their feet would carry them. I couldn't hold my laughter.

"You think that's funny, huh?" Heaven said, giving me a shove as she sat up in bed.

She looked beat. Last night was a long one. Almost an all nighter. Since we started having sex, it seemed like every time our bodies met, it got better. And the carton of eggnog and cognac only added to it. Sex with Heaven was like getting a slice of heaven. Since I had been with her, I had forgotten all about Sapphire. Sapphire who?

"Yeah, a little bit. They remind me of me and my brother when we were kids."

Heaven gave me a funny look.

"I never told you about him, huh?"

Her gray eyes becoming cloudy. "Do you remember anything from the night you beat up Whisper?"

"What are you talking about?" I asked, wondering how we went from talking about my brother to her old pimp.

"Do you remember anything you talked about when you drove me home?"

I thought for a moment. The incident was almost three weeks ago. Nothing came to mind. "Nah. I don't remember nothing after the liquor kicked in."

Heaven had an eerie look in her eyes. "You were—"

"Mommy, c'mon!" Mason yelled, popping up in the doorway.

The look disappeared from Heaven's eyes. "Okay. Here we come. I'll tell you later. Grab your phone so you can record them opening presents," she said, kissing me and getting out of bed.

I had a bunch of questions floating around in my head but when the blanket fell to the bed, revealing her nakedness, I went dumb. Every time I seen her body, I was mesmerized. Like a hypnotist put me under a spell. At twenty six years old, her 36DD breasts still held onto a little bit of their perkiness. The sag was minimal at best. Her skin was a cocoa butter complexion, her areolas large and the color of chocolate milk. And even though she never worked out a day in her life, her stomach was flat, arms and legs sculpted. Her hips to waist ratio looked unreal. Like a something out of a comic book. And then there was her butt. It was absolutely flawless. I had examined it thoroughly and didn't find a single bump, blemish, stretch mark, or wrinkle. When booty was looked up in the dictionary, Webster should have a picture of Heaven's backside as a reference. And it currently had me stuck as it clapped and jiggled while she walked over to the closet. I was having so much fun watching it bounce that I got a little disappointed when she slid into her robe.

"What?" She asked when she seen me watching her.

"Do you know that for the first time in my life I can tell a woman that she is perfect and really mean it?"

She smiled and blushed. "Thank you, baby. And you are the perfect man."

"I knew that since I could walk. Shoot, Adam didn't look this good," I laughed, flexing my arms.

She laughed and threw a robe at me. "Okay, Mr. Perfect. Get dressed before the twins come back with a problem."

"Do you want to open your gift or wait until later?" I asked nonchalantly while sliding into the robe.

She looked surprised. "You got me a gift?"

"We got you a gift. Look in the closet. Top shelf. All the way in the back."

Her eyes flashed with excitement as she began digging through the closet. Then, she started screaming. "Ahhh! Oh my God!"

"You okay, baby?"

Heaven started trembling as she held the jewelry box. "Open it."

"Y'all good?" Ray asked, appearing at the door.

The twins were standing next to him, all of them wearing looks of concern.

"She just found her present," I explained.

"What is it?" She asked, her gray eyes sparkling with excitement as she stared at the box. "Open it, mommy!" Jason yelled.

Heaven's hands shook as she pulled the ribbon from the jewelry box. Inside was a thirty five millimeter platinum heart pendant covered in crushed diamonds with an 18" chain. Inscribed on the back was: We love you more than everything you've ever been through. Love Robert, Ray, Jason & Mason.

"It's beautiful!" Heaven cried. "I love it so much. Thanks, guys."

I took it from her. "Let me put it on you."

"It's pretty, mommy," Mason said.

"Thank you baby," she said before turning to me. "Are you ready for your gift?"

I didn't even try to act modest. "Hell yeah!"

She went over to the drawer and pulled a gray box. I knew from the shape that a watch was inside. Me, Ray, and the twins 'ooohed and ahhhed' when I opened it. Inside was a gold Aqua Master watch.

"Oh, hell yeah!" I smiled. "Wait till my boys see this!"

After going through all the presents under the tree with Jason, Mason, and Ray, we had breakfast and spent the rest of the morning making videos of the boys playing with their toys. Around noon we piled into my Regal and headed to my parents' house. During the drive, me and Ray talked about the

NBA and our Milwaukee Bucks, the twins had their faces in their tablets, and Heaven was silently biting her fingernails.

"Stop it," I said, grabbing her hand and holding onto it.

"Babe, I'm nervous. I never met anyone's parents before."

I took my eyes off the road to look at her. "My parents are cool, baby. They will love you. Trust me. Stop worrying."

"Worry is a sin, mama. Jesus said don't worry," Mason cut in.

Now that was funny, and cute, and gave us a much needed laugh. When we got to my parents' house, I led the way. Heaven held my hand, and Ray and the twins brought up the rear. The door was unlocked so I let us in. Deliciousness tickled my nose as soon as I walked in the door. My dad was sitting in the chair in front of the TV. His face lit up when we walked in the house

"Hey son!"

Even though he was sick, Pop looked good. No oxygen machine trailing behind him and he didn't look fragile or weak. He looked healthy and virulent. He wore olive green slacks, an ugly tan Christmas sweater, and loafers. I could tell my mom dressed him.

"Hey, pop!" I greeted him with a hug.

"Merry Christmas, son! Glad y'all could make it. And you must be Heaven?" He asked, stepping back to look her over.

"Yes," she blushed. "It's nice to meet you, Mr. Johnson. Merry Christmas."

"Merry Christmas to you, too. You have a beautiful family," he told her before turning to me. "I'da left Bey in the desert, son."

Me and Pop laughed at the inside joke.

"And your name is?" Pop asked, sizing up Ray and sticking out his hand.

"Ray," the man child answered, maintaining eye contact with my father as they shook hands.

"I served in the military with a man named Ray. He was a good man. You a good man, Ray?"

"Yes, I am." He nodded. "Merry Christmas."

Pop smiled. "Merry Christmas to you too, son. Nice to meet you." Then, he turned to the twins. "Hey, little guys! These are some handsome boys you have here, Heaven. Look just like Robert and Roger when they were little."

I saw heaven tense up a little when my father mentioned me and my brother.

"Thank you, Mr. Johnson. They are my angels."

"Anna! Come on in here. Sledge and the gang are here!" My father called.

While my mother made her way to greet us, I took everyone's coats and shoes.

"Hey, Robert! Oh, the babies are so cute! Wow, they look just like my Roger and Robert when they were babies. Hi, Heaven! You are just too beautiful! And Ray, how many hearts have you broken?" My mother gushed, floating around to give everyone hugs. "Merry Christmas. C'mon and sit down. Basketball is on. You boys can stay up front while I put the finishing touches on this food. Heaven, would you help me?"

I gave Heaven a wave as she went to the kitchen with my mother. "This is our season to win it all again pop. Giannis can't be stopped," I said as I sat down to watch Christmas basketball.

Pop just stared at me. The look in his eyes told me that he didn't care what I said about basketball. Then, he smiled and gave me a nod. I knew the gesture was more than it seemed. He was letting me know that he was proud of me and I had done good. That small gesture made me feel good. Having dad's approval meant everything. I acknowledged his gesture with a smile of my own.

"Yeah, son. I agree. We're the best team in the NBA. This is our year."

Chapter 26

Heaven

As soon as I seen Mr. Johnson, something inside me twitched. Robert's father was handsome. Tall, dark, and bald. His eyes were dark brown and serious. And when I looked into his face, it was like looking into older versions of Jason and Mason. My kids were light skinned versions of Robert's father and it scared the hell out of me. I tried to look calm on the outside while following Mrs. Johnson into the kitchen but on the inside I was freaking out. "It is so nice to finally meet you, Heaven. Robert has told me so much about you. Can you cook?"

"I know my way around the kitchen but I can't do all of this," I admitted looking around the kitchen in awe.

There was food spread out around the kitchen. It seemed like every inch of counter and table space was filled with bowls and pans of food. I had never seen one person cook so much. Corn bread, macaroni casserole, greens, yams, apple pie, peach cobbler, ham, smothered chicken, fried chicken, and dressing.

"This is for Christmas dinner," she grinned. "I love to cook and I go all out during the holidays. Can you check those greens for me?"

I walked over to a pot of greens on the stove. "Do you think we'll be able to eat all of this?" "No, baby," she laughed. "We're going to have our fill and then I'll give the rest to the church. Do it every year."

I liked Robert's mother. She was nice and homely. Had that southern hospitality. And she was pretty. Reminded me of a healthier Vanessa Williams. Blue eyes and all. And when I say healthy, I meant good weight. Curvy and filled out in all the right places. How a woman is supposed to be.

"Robert tells me you're into poetry," she said while cutting up the ham.

"Yes. I write and recite spoken word."

"That's really nice. Have you heard Robert sing?"

"Yes. He is good. One of the best singers I've ever heard. I'm his biggest fan."

"Amen. He has the voice of an angel and won't even use his gift. I—"

I watched Mrs. Johnson's lips moving but I didn't hear anything she was saying. I couldn't stop thinking about how much the twins looked like her husband. I didn't remember sleeping with Mr. Johnson but apparently I did. Furthermore, how was I going to explain this to Robert and his mother? They would probably kick me out of their lives and Robert would hate me. Just when I thought I'd found the love of my life, it had to come with a heavy price. I was going to need to test his family to see if they were a match to give my kids the bone marrow transplant.

"And I just love it!" Mrs. Johnson said and began laughing.

I didn't know what she was laughing about but I laughed with her. We continued talking while putting the finishing touches on the food and putting it onto trays and serving dishes. Then, we began taking it into the dining room where she showed me how to set the table. I looked around the dining room while I brought out dishes. It was beautiful. A crystal chandelier hung from the ceiling. A big picture window allowed us to see the snow falling outside. The long granite table looked big enough to seat eight people. On the wall were a few shelves that held family mementos and memorabilia. Pictures, trophies, and certificates. I stopped to look. When I saw the picture of Robert and Roger, I almost dropped the dish.

"Careful, honey!" Mrs. Johnson said as she walked into the dining room carrying the ham. "Kinda slippery. I, um, I'll be right back," I mumbled before sitting the dish on the table and dashing to the bathroom.

As soon as the door closed, I began hyperventilating. I couldn't believe my luck. Out of all the families in Wisconsin I ended up spending Christmas with the Johnsons. When Mr. and Mrs. Johnson said my kids looked like her son, I thought they were just being nice. I had heard that so many times. People always said my kids looked like such and such. But in this case, it was true. When I seen the picture of Roger, it was like looking at my kids brother. Or father. A knock on the door interrupted my panic attack.

"Heaven, are you okay?" Mrs. Johnson called.

"Yes. I, um, just need a minute."

"Are you sure?"

"Yes ma'am. I'm fine. I'll be out in a second."

I turned on the cold water and splashed my face. That helped. I could breathe again and had calmed down but in my head I was still freaking out. I took a few more moments to gather myself before leaving the bathroom. When I walked back in the kitchen, Mrs. Johnson was giving me the eye.

"Are you okay?" She asked, staring at me like she was trying to read my mind.

"Yes. I'm good. Do you want me to take the cornbread out there?" I asked, avoiding her gaze. She paused like she wanted to say something more but let it go. "Yes. Take the cornbread, please."

I grabbed that pan and got away from her as fast as I could. I didn't want to stand in her presence too long. She had that motherly stare that could see through people and I didn't want her to figure out what was going on in my head before I had the chance to figure it out on my own. When the table was finally set, Mrs. Johnson called everyone to eat.

"You good, baby?" Robert asked as he pulled his chair next to mine.

"Yes. I'm fine. Ready to eat," I said, giving him what I hoped was an Oscar worthy smile. He turned his attention to the food. "Yeah. Looks good. Mama is the best cook in the world!" After Mr. Johnson said a prayer over the food, we dug into the meal fit for kings. We talked, laughed, and swapped stories while eating. The food was delicious but I didn't have an appetite. I nibbled at the food while giving fake smiles and laughs. I tried to push my brooding thoughts to the back of my head and enjoy the Christmas spirit like everyone else at the table, but I couldn't. There were way too many thoughts running around my head. On the one hand, I had found my kids' father and it looked like they would get the operation. That was a blessing. But the other hand revealed despair. Despair I wasn't ready to deal with. I was trapped in these thoughts when I felt someone watching me. I looked up as Mrs. Johnson looked away. She was slick. And she was also suspicious of me. A few moments later, my suspicions were confirmed when I caught her sneaking peaks from her husband to the twins. I hoped this didn't get ugly. After dinner, the men and boys went back to the living room while I helped Mrs. Johnson clean up. The vibe between us had changed. It was strained. Like she knew my secret.

"So, are the twins close with their father?" she asked as we piled dishes into the sink. "It seems like they really like Robert."

I didn't know how to answer the question. I didn't want to tell her the twins never met their father because I used to be a hoe. Or that I found their father as soon as I stepped into her home. I also didn't want to lie to her. "I don't know where he is. I haven't seen him in years. But we've been talking about me all day. Aren't you tired of asking me questions? How about I ask you some so I can get to know you. Where do you go to church? What do you do for a living?"

Mrs. Johnson eyed me suspiciously as she shoved a pan into the dishwasher. She knew I was trying to deflect and keep the conversation off me. "We go to a small church. Saint

Mary's Missionary Baptist Church over on 46th and Burleigh. Been going there for almost twenty years. What about you?"

"I go to a small non-denominational church in West Allis. I chose non-denominational because I didn't want to get into the politics of religion. How did you and your husband meet?"

A smile spread across her face. "We met back in college. Love at first sight. I knew on our first date that I was going to marry Freddy. And a few years later, I became his bride. When we had our boys, our family was completed. So, does twins run in your family like it does in mine?"

Mrs. Johnson was good. She had flipped the spot light back to me, forcing an answer. "I'm not sure. I don't know much about my family's history. My mother died while I was young and I know nothing of my father's family. But can we talk about something else? It's kind of upsetting to think about my broken family and I don't want to be crying on Christmas. We're supposed to be celebrating Jesus," I said, letting out a small laugh.

She looked like she wanted to protest, but didn't. Instead, she gave an *'I'm on to you'* eye before switching subjects. When the dishes were done, I got ahold of Robert and told him I was ready to leave. A few minutes later, we were all dressed in our coats standing at the door. I couldn't wait to get out of that house. I needed some space and time to think.

"It was really nice to meet you, Mr. Johnson," I smiled, giving Robert's father a hug.

"It was nice to meet you too, Heaven. Merry Christmas and Happy New Year."

When Mr. Johnson walked over to say his goodbyes to the boys, Mrs. Johnson approached, a knowing look in her eyes. "It was really nice to meet you, Mrs. Johnson. And thanks for the food. You are an amazing cook."

"It was my pleasure, sweety," she smiled, opening her arms for a hug. When we were cheek to cheek she began whispering. "You don't have to be a stranger anymore, Heaven. We're family now."

Chapter 27

Robert

My eyes shot open as I sat up in bed. Sweat covered my body. I was hot like I had been in a sauna.

"You okay, baby?" Heaven asked, rubbing my back. I couldn't talk.

"Was it a bad dream?"

I nodded. But it was more than a bad dream. It was a nightmare way worse than the one on Elm Street.

"You want to talk about it?"

I really didn't want to talk about it. I wanted to roll over and go back to sleep. But I couldn't. Every time I closed my eyes, I seen his eyes. "I need to tell you something," I mumbled when I found my voice.

"What is it?" She asked, her voice trembling with concern.

I didn't want to tell her, but I had to get it off my chest. This was my deepest secret. And every Christmas it haunted me the most. "I killed my twin brother, Roger."

Boom! I had finally gotten it off my chest. Had finally told someone other than my parents and my boys.

"I know."

I looked at her over my shoulder. "What do you mean, *'you know'*?"

"You told me the night you got drunk. The night you beat up Whisper."

I couldn't believe what I was hearing. All this time I was worried about her finding out and she already knew. "Why didn't you tell me you knew?"

"I was going to tell you yesterday morning but the kids wanted to open their presents."

We became silent. I wanted her to know the truth. That I wasn't a killer. "It was an accident."

"What happened? Is that what you were dreaming about?"

"It was an accident," I repeated. "I had just bought an old, restored Firebird. The car was real fast. Me and Roger were taking it for a spin. I was showing off and burning rubber around every corner. Doing donuts in the middle of the intersection. Just acting a fool. I was high out of my mind and really in no condition to drive, let alone do stunts. Roger didn't drink or smoke. He was straight as an arrow. Participated in all sports. Got good grades. Was in college to be a lawyer. I was the reject. The black sheep. I stayed in drama with my parents because they hated my lifestyle.

"Well, I was speeding down Marion, a side street off Capitol. I had just blown through a stop sign and when I looked over, I seen fear on Roger's face. He yelled for me to slow down. I didn't. His fear excited me. Made me go faster. Made me want to try a stunt. The stop sign got bigger as we neared the end of the block. I was supposed to be slowing down but my foot hadn't touched the brake pedal. There was a busy intersection on the other side of the stop sign. I thought that if I got up enough speed, that I could dodge through the heavy traffic like they did in the movies.

"Roger was screaming for me to slow down but I was committed. And by the time I blew through the stop sign, I was doing about eighty miles an hour. I just missed a car going east, crossed the center line, and almost made it to the other side of the intersection when a car clipped my bumper. The Firebird flipped in the air, twisting and tumbling like the race cars at NASCAR. We clipped a few cars before the Firebird wedged itself into a parked station wagon.

"I was dazed and confused and bleeding out the side of my face. Also broke a few bones. When I finally found my bearing, I looked for Roger. He was in the passenger seat shaking like he was having a seizure. I called his name but he

188

didn't respond. Just kept shaking. That's when I noticed the blood. It was everywhere. I looked him over and seen that he was hurt bad. The passenger door sliced through him. Cut him in half. Literally severed his torso from his hips. I screamed until the police and paramedics came. They cut us from the car and I got arrested for drunk driving and vehicular homicide. Got five years."

"Oh my God, Robert! That is so terrible. I am so sorry," Heaven said, wrapping me in a hug and kissing my neck.

"I am too. That's why me and my dad stopped talking. He blamed me. Said I killed his son. Roger was his favorite. We're paternal twins. Roger looked just like him. I favor my mother."

"It was an accident, baby. You're father said it out of hurt. I'm sure he didn't mean it."

"Nah, Pop was right. I've accepted that I killed Roger. It was my fault. If I wouldn't have been driving recklessly, Roger would still be here."

"You can't put that pressure or burden on yourself. God's plan is perfect. Everything that's supposed to happen is what happens."

"So you saying that God killed my brother?"

"I'm not saying that. Roger died because it was his time to go. You're still here because it wasn't your time. God is in control of everything and uses everything to show his glory and power. I think you've been looking at the accident wrong. You keep looking at what you lost instead of what you've gained. The accident changed you. It made you a better person. You educated yourself and now use what you learned to help future generations through your speeches. Roger's death wasn't in vain. You are saving other kids' lives."

Hearing Heaven's perspective on the accident gave me something to think about. I wasn't sure if I believed everything she said, but I was using his death to try to save other kids lives. "I needed to hear that, baby. Thanks."

"That's what your woman is supposed to do. Now come here and lie down with me and listen to my new poem. Tell me what you think."

Chapter 28

Heaven

I opened my eyes and found Robert's side of the bed empty. He probably just went to the bathroom. I grabbed my phone to check the time. 6:54 AM. As I lay in bed, I thought about the accident and death of Roger. It was horrific. I couldn't imagine walking around carrying a burden like that. Made me feel like the secrets I kept from him were nothing. He would have to walk around for the rest of his life knowing that he was responsible for his brother's death. That was terrible.

Then, there was my good/bad news. I still wasn't sure how I was going to tell him that I found the twins father. After we left his parent's house yesterday, I spent most of the evening considering his possible reactions. Narrowed it down to two. Happy or mad. I hoped that he would be happy. Hoped that he would chalk the misdeed up to my past and we would continue our love story. But there was only one way to find out for sure and that was to tell him. I decided to tell him when he came back in the room.

After five minutes of waiting and he didn't show up, I went to look for him. Ended up searching the whole house only to realize he was gone. That surprised me. It wasn't like him to leave without telling me. I got a strange feeling in my gut. Like something was wrong. I went to grab my phone and called him. It went right to voicemail. I left a short message before sending a text. Then, I waited. When my phone rang a few minutes later I got excited, hoping it was him but it was Reesy.

"Hey," I answered dryly.

"Hey love. You okay? Why do you sound down the day after Christmas?"

"You wouldn't believe the night I just had. I don't think there are words to describe it."

"You know what, Heaven? The reason I called is because I knew something was wrong. I could feel it. Two minutes ago I was in a dead sleep but God woke me up and put it on my heart to call you. What's going on?"

I took a deep breath before spilling the beans. "I found the twins' father."

"What? Oh my God! That is great news, honey! When did you find out? Who is he?"

"Roger."

"Roger? Who is he? I don't remember you telling me about a guy named Roger."

"That's because I never told you about him. I didn't even know who he was until yesterday. Its Robert's twin brother."

"What!? Robert has a twin brother? And you slept with him?"

"Yes. Well, he had a twin brother. He died. Robert kind of got him killed."

"Wait, Heaven. This is sounding crazy. Robert killed his own brother?"

"Not on purpose. It was an accident. He died in a crash. Robert was driving."

"Oh, my God, Heaven! All this is too much for one morning. I haven't even had my coffee yet. So, how do you know that Roger is their father?"

"Because I saw a picture of him yesterday and they look exactly like him. And his mother knows, I think."

"And how does she know?"

"When I saw the picture of Roger, I almost fainted and she noticed. I also caught her looking at her husband and the twins during dinner. They look just like Mr. Johnson. At first I thought he was the father until I seen the picture of Roger."

"This is the wildest thing I've ever heard, love. God has blessed you in a mighty way. Out of all the men in

Milwaukee and you meet Robert. Of all the families in Milwaukee and you end up spending Christmas with his. Don't you see, Heaven? God orchestrated this. He is so faithful and good. He answered our prayers in a way that we never could've imagined. His ways are not our ways."

The weight of it all dawned on me at that moment. God had provided. "I can't even explain how blessed and grateful I feel."

"So, when are you going to tell him?"

"I was going to tell him this morning but I woke up and he was gone."

"This is so much of a blessing, Heaven. We couldn't have predicted a better ending to this."

My phone vibrated from another call. I didn't 't recognize the number. "Hang on for a second, Reesy. Somebody is on my other line. It might be Robert. Let me call you back."

"Okay, sweety. God is so good! Bless you, lord!"

I clicked over to answer the new call. "Hello?"

"Hello? Heaven?"

My heart sank when I heard her voice. "Yes, this is me. Um... Hi."

"Good morning. How are you doing? This is Mrs. Johnson. Robert's mother."

"I'm fine. Just got up. I was looking for Robert. Has he called you? I was kind of worried about him. He left without telling me."

"Don't worry about him. He's fine. He always goes through these spells around Christmas time. He's carrying a lot of weight on his shoulders. I spoke to him a little while ago. He gave me your phone number."

I didn't know what to say after that. I wanted to know why she got my number. This wasn't a social call. "Oh. Okay,"

"The reason I called you is because we need to talk. Woman to woman."

She had figured it out. "About what?"

"Not like this. Face to face. Give me your address."

I gave her my information and she said she was on her way. I didn't know what to do with myself while waiting for Mrs. Johnson to show up. I sat on the couch and watched YouTube videos, chewed my nails, bit my lips, and twirled my fingers through my hair. Fifty three minutes later, my doorbell rang. I put on my best smile and answered.

"Good morning, Mrs. Johnson."

She greeted me with an icy look, fire and anger swirling in her blue eyes. "Good morning," she said tersely. "May I come in?"

Why was she angry? What did I do? How would this end? Just relax, Heaven. See it through. "Yes. Come in," I said, stepping aside to let her in.

"Can I get your coat?"

"I'll keep my coat."

"Okay. Are you angry with me? Did I do something wrong?"

If looks could kill, I would be on my way to join the Lord. "How long have you been sleeping with my husband?"

The question threw me for a loop. It was the last thing I expected to hear and for a moment I was stuck. "Excuse me?"

"Are those my husband's kids?"

I was still trying to process it all. Then, I remembered how she was looking at Mr. Johnson and the twins. She thought I slept with her husband because they looked like him and Roger.

"No, Mrs. Johnson. They are not your husband's kids," I laughed, shaking my head.

She got angrier. "You think this is a game, child? You think sleeping with a married man is funny?".

I took a step back just in case she tried something. "No, Mrs. Johnson. I don't think it's funny. And I didn't sleep with your husband. I slept with Roger."

I watched as she unwrapped her mind around me sleeping with her husband and rewrapped it around me sleeping with her son. Both of them. The anger vanished, replaced by confusion. "You mean those are my grandbabies?"

I nodded. "Yes. I think. I didn't sleep with your husband."

Her eyes went from stormy to clear blue. "Oh, I'm so sorry, Heaven! I thought..." She paused, lost for words as the gravity of it all became clearer. "I'm sorry. Does Robert know?"

"No. I just found out yesterday and I wasn't sure how to tell him."

"In the dining room, when you almost dropped the food, that's when you found out? When you saw his picture?"

"Yes."

Excitement lit her eyes. "Oh my goodness! I had it all wrong. Can we sit down? May I have something to drink?"

"Yes. Come in the kitchen."

I grabbed two bottles of water, offering her one as we sat at the table.

"Tell me how you met Roger."

I really didn't want to open up that chapter of my life to Robert's mother. I didn't want to be judged.

"It's okay, Heaven. I won't judge you. As a mother, I need to know."

When she said that, I knew I would have to tell me the truth. "We met at a college party, or something like that. Back then I was wild. Roger approached me and we hit it off. I don't remember much because I had been drinking and doing drugs. Before the night was over we... You know. And that was the first and last time I seen him."

Mrs. Johnson just stared at me. Then, she got up and hugged me. When her arms wrapped around me, it felt like what I imagined a mother's embrace was supposed to feel like. She was warm and smelled good. Then, all the years of searching for my kids' father hit me and I started crying. The humiliation from testing so many men, the thousands of dollars spent on tests, the sleepless nights worried if my kids would live to see their next birthday. It was all over.

"I don't care what you were or what you did, Heaven. It doesn't matter to me. What matters is that you love my son and he loves you. And that those babies are taken care of. We all have a past, dear. And I won't judge you by yours. I can't. But I will love you."

Her words were so kind and caring. Reminded me of Reesy. "I need to test you and Mr. Johnson. Not only for a DNA test, but also to see if one of you are a match."

She frowned. "A match for what?"

"They have Acute Lymphocytic Leukemia and need a bone marrow transplant."

Her eyes grew wide. "Oh my Lord! Poor babies! Of course, Heaven. We will do it as soon as possible."

"Mommy, I'm hungry," Mason whined, walking into the kitchen wiping sleep from his eyes. When he seen Mrs. Johnson, his face lit up. "Hi, Mrs. Johnson! Do you have some more peach cobbler?"

"Good morning, sweetheart. And you can have all the peach cobbler you want, on one condition."

Mason looked like he was ready to give her all the toys in his closet. "What?"

"That you call me Granny."

He looked to me seeking my approval. I nodded.

"Okay, Granny!" He yelled excitedly.

"Do you mind if I cook breakfast, Heaven?" She asked.

196

Images of the Christmas dinner popped into my head. "Of course not, Mrs. Johnson. My kitchen is your kitchen."

She gave me a raised eyebrow. "No, sweetheart. I'm no longer Mrs. Johnson. Call me mom, okay?"

I wasn't going to argue with that.

Chapter 29

Robert

I stared down at Roger's granite headstone, emotions rolling through my body in waves. Eight years passed since his death but it was still hard for me to accept that he was gone. Picturing him lying in the dirt was even harder.

"What's up, Hammer? I was having trouble sleeping. It always happens to me around this time of year. I keep seeing your face every time I close my eyes. I didn't know what else to do so I thought I would come talk to you. I know I should've been come around but... Man, I never wanted to picture you in a hole in the ground. It's still hard for me to accept that you gone. I always ask God why he didn't take me instead. I know they say God don't make mistakes but... I don't know.

"I wish you were here, man. This has been a crazy year. Me and Pop patched things up last time we were here. I hate that it took him about to die to squash our beef. But the bright side is, at least we got all the petty stuff behind us. He says he only got about a year left. I hope that y'all get to be together. I got arrested a little while back, too. Had to beat up a pimp. Never thought that I would be in that situation but something good came out of it. Having the fight made me realize that I was in love. Her name is Heaven. She's a huge upgrade from Sapphire. Got twin sons that remind me of us when we were little. I told her about you and she believes everything happens for a reason. She told me to stop looking at what I lost and instead focus on what I've gained. Even though you leaving made me change, it's hard to see any gain because nothing I can do or have done will fill the hole you left in all of our hearts and lives. I know what she said has some truth to it, but its still hard to see anything good coming out of this because I would give up everything I own to have you back for just one minute. I don't know, brah."

My words seemed to fail me so I stood there staring at the headstone. When I was tired of standing, I sat on the snow covered grave as memories of our childhood played in my head. The tears came like water rushing from a broken dam. I didn't know how long I sat there crying, but when I finished grieving, a perfect peace washed over me. I couldn't describe the feeling with words. All I knew was that I felt comforted. Like everything was going to be okay. And then I thought about Heaven. I knew she was probably worried about me.

"I'm sorry, Roger. For everything. I gotta go. Gotta get back to Heaven and the kids. I know she's probably worried about me because I left without telling her. But don't worry, man. I won't be a stranger. I love you."

When I pulled up to Heaven's house, I got the surprise of my life. My mother's car was parked out front. I assumed the worst. Something must have happened to Pop! After parking, I ran towards the house like I was Usain Bolt. When I burst through the door, the first thing I noticed was the smell. Mom had been cooking.

"Mom? Heaven?" I called, walking through the living room.

"We're in the kitchen!" Heaven called.

I walked in and seen mom, Heaven, Jason, Mason, and Ray all sitting at the table eating breakfast. Everything looked normal.

"What's going on?" I asked, looking back and forth from my mom to Heaven.

Mom looked at me with the smile of someone getting a birthday present. "Everything is fine, son. Sit down and have some breakfast."

Heaven got up and motioned for me to have her seat.

"So what's the occasion, mom? Why are you here this early the day after Christmas? I didn't know you knew where Heaven lived."

"Relax, Robert. Have some bacon and give me a kiss," Heaven said, giving me a peck on the lips before sitting on my lap.

I took a piece of bacon off her plate and eyed my mom, waiting for her answer.

"I came to visit my grandkids."

She acted like the simple answer was supposed to quench my desire to know why she was at Heaven's house. It didn't. And I was about to pester her with more questions when I noticed the way she was looking at Jason and Mason. I missed something. I looked to Heaven for an answer and seen she was wearing the same gift receiving smile as mom. "Will somebody tell me what's going on?"

"Your brother is Jason and Mason's father," Heaven said.

My heart skipped a beat. Ray dropped his fork, and Jason and Mason stared at their mother with the same look I was giving her. I searched her face to make sure I heard her correctly. She looked happy. Her gray eyes sparking and clear.

"What did you say?"

She looked into my eyes and repeated herself. Slowly. "Robert, Roger is the twins' father."

It felt like I had been hit in the head with a bag of puzzle pieces. "What? How? When did... What?"

"Yesterday when we were at your parents' house, I seen a picture of Roger. They look just like him. Look."

My eyes went from Heaven to the twins. Jason and Mason were identical. At first glance, it was hard to tell one from the other but I knew who was who. And as I stared at them, studying their faces, I noticed they looked exactly like Roger. So much so that I didn't know how I missed the resemblance.

"But how do you know for sure?" I asked.

"Because I said so," my mother cut in. "Now quit asking so many questions. Now is not the time for that. This is a time for celebrating. Roger left a piece of himself in the world and let's just be thankful."

Chapter 30

Robert

"Oh snaps! This is my song!" I yelled when R. Kelly's 'Hey Mr. DJ' began playing. "Come on, baby. Let's dance," I told Heaven, snatching her away from Queesha, Vito's girl.

"What you know about this?" Heaven asked, wrapping her arms around my shoulders. "Girl, I was bumping and grinding to R. Kelly when you was still in middle school."

She rolled her eyes. "Whatever, old man."

I pulled her close to me and whispered in her ear. "I got yo' old man. Meet me in the bathroom and I'll show you how old I am."

"Stop being nasty," she laughed. "We're out with friends. Wait til we get home, mannish old man."

After the light banter, she lay her head against my chest and we slow danced to the music. As I held her in my arms, I thought about how happy I'd been since she had come into my life. She completed me. She was my best friend. I loved her with all my heart. And in a few moments, I would make it official.

"Excuse me! Can I get everybody's attention?"

I looked around and seen Junior standing on a table tapping a fork against his champagne flute. "I just wanted to thank everybody for coming out to celebrate Valentine's Day with me and my girl. I—"

"Any time you serving free drinks, I'm there," Mike cut in, toasting a glass of champagne with a big breasted woman named Kamala.

"Next year it's on you, Mike. I heard Kamala been talking babies with Heaven so you better be ready."

Mike turned to his date, his face serious. "What the hell he talking about?"

We all bust out laughing.

"I'm playing, Mike. But seriously, I just want to thank everybody for coming out to share this evening with me and my Julie. Hopefully we can do this every year," Junior said, toasting a glass of champagne with his new flame.

When the rest of the party goers began toasting with their dates and significant others, I took my cue. "Hold on, everybody. Before we all go back to moving and grooving, I got a few things that I want to say."

Everyone gave me their attention. Mom, dad, Reesy and her husband Terry, Vito and Queesha, Mike and Kamala, Junior and Julie.

"I just wanted to say a few words to all the beautiful couples in the house tonight. This is a beautiful evening and I love being able to share it with you beautiful people."

"You bet not cry, nigga!" Mike shouted.

Everyone shot him daggers.

"I want to thank Junior and Julie for coming up with the idea to get together and celebrate this day of love and for renting this suite for us to chill in. Next year it's on me. And I wanna thank my boys Vito, Jr, and Mike for not only being my best friends, but also my brothers. After Roger died, God used you brothers to restore the relationship three fold. To my mom and dad, thank y'all for loving me when I was unlovable. Thank y'all for mending my wounds and coming together to give me and Roger life. And thank y'all most of all for showing me what true love looks like."

Then, I turned to Heaven. "And Heaven, thank you for my nephews who I will raise as sons. When Roger died, I was devastated. I never thought that I would see him again. But thanks to you, I get to wake up every day and see his face in Jason and Mason. God don't make mistakes, baby. Thank you also for letting me experience true love, for loving me in spite of my flaws, and keeping all my secrets. And trusting me with yours. Not only have you brought an unspeakable joy to my life, but you've made me a better person. And I know without a doubt that I want to spend the rest of my life with you. So,"

I paused to pull the ring box from my pocket and get down on one knee. I heard gasps from our friends and loved ones.

"Heaven Marie Choeun, will you make me the happiest man in the world and be my wife?" Heaven's body began to tremble when I opened the ring box. Inside was a gold three carat diamond ring. I stared up into her tear filled gray eyes awaiting an answer to my proposal. She didn't say anything. Just stared at me without blinking. The seconds began to expand and it felt like I had been on one knee for a full minute.

"For heaven's sake, girl! Say something!" Reesy said.

Her mouth opened, but no words came out. But her tear ducts worked just fine. Tears spilled down her face as she shook her head up and down. Everyone cheered as I slid the ring onto her finger. And as I looked at her hand, I couldn't help but think that the ring belonged there. When I stood, she attacked my lips with a long passionate kiss.

"Yes, baby! Yes, I'll marry you," she said after we came up for air.

The rest of the evening was spent riding on cloud nine. When the shindig was over, me and Heaven left with Reesy and Terry. We had come off the elevator and were walking through the hotel lobby when I heard a voice that sent a chill up my spine.

"Robert!"

My heart sank so far to the pit of my stomach that I thought I would need surgery to put it back on the left side of my chest. I wanted to run and hide, but couldn't. That would be weak. So instead, I turned to face her.

"What's up, Sapphire?"

"Oh, hell nah, nigga! Where the fuck you been and who is this bitch!?" Sapphire cursed, wobbling towards me wearing a tight red dress and heels. She had a lady friend in tow. Both looked tipsy.

"Robert?" Heaven questioned, squeezing my hand and looking up at me.

"That's Sapphire," I mumbled.

A fire as hot as hell burned behind her gray eyes.

"Nigga, do you hear me talking to you? How you gonna disrespect me like this?" Sapphire continued as she got closer.

"Don't start nothing up in here. I know about Mike and Junior I moved on. You do you and I'ma do me."

Her eyes grew wide with alarm. "Wait, Robert! They didn't mean nothing to me, baby. They lying. Let's go somewhere and talk. I need you. The boys need you," she whined.

"We don't got nothing to talk about. I already told you it's over. What's done is done. I moved on. This is my fiancé, Heaven."

Sapphire looked to Heaven, instant hate flashing in her eyes. "Hell nah, Robert! You ain't leaving me!"

She reached out to grab me but Heaven stepped in front of me. My fiancé's beautiful face had changed into as mask of fury. "Keep your hands off my man!" Heaven yelled, yanking Sapphire's hand from my arm.

"Oh, hell nah! Bitch, no you didn't just put yo' hands on me! Robert is my man. I don't play that shit!" Sapphire screamed, kicking off her heels and rushing Heaven.

I wasn't about to let the drama queen beat up Heaven so I grabbed Sapphire around the waist, lifting her off her feet. "Ay girl, chill!"

"Let me go, Robert!" Sapphire thrashed around.

I looked to Terry and Reesy for help but they didn't budge. Terry looked amused and Reesy wore a smirk. Like she wanted me to let them fight. But I knew Heaven would lose. Sapphire was wild and she had a buddy for back up.

"Get out of the way, Robert. Let her go," Heaven said. "God is going to have to forgive me because I'm about to beat her ass."

If the situation wasn't so serious I would have laughed. I never heard Heaven curse or seen her so mad. But I held it together, waiting for Reesy or Terry to intervene. They didn't. Terry looked like he was ringside at a boxing match and Reesy still wore the smirk. I gave her a pleading look, hoping Heaven's angel would do something angelic. She didn't. So I let Sapphire go. She charged Heaven, her hands flying in all directions like a windmill. I knew she was about to rip my new fiancé to shreds. But before Sapphire could reach my girl, Heaven side stepped the windmill and a hard right cross landed right on Sapphire's jaw. The Laila Ali move caught everyone off guard, especially Sapphire. My fake baby mama went down in a puddle of flesh and bones. I was in awe. I had seen my fair share of knockouts and this was easily in the top five. I was proud of my girl for delivering the one hitter quitter.

"Damn, girl!" I yelled.

"Down goes Frazier!" Terry laughed.

The hotel staff gathered around the commotion. I expected them to be on the phones calling the police. To my surprise, no one moved. Just stared to see if the fight was over. And when they realized Sapphire was done, they went back to work.

"Let's go, y'all," Reesy said, leading the way through the glass double doors.

I wrapped my arm around Heaven's waist and led her outside, smiling like a proud father that just watched his daughter do the impossible. "Damn, baby. I didn't know you had that in you,"

"She was all talk, baby. Most people that talk loud can't fight. But I'll fight for what's mine." Yep. She was the one.

Epilogue

Christmas is upon us again and a lot has changed within the past year. For starters, Heaven and I got married. Tied the knot on July 4th and spent the honeymoon in Jamaica. Since we got married, every day can only be described with one word. Magical. We're also adding an addition to our family in three months. Heaven is six months pregnant with our daughter. I'm looking forward to raising all of our children. Jason and Mason are doing fine. Mom was a perfect match for them to get that bone marrow transplant. They had the operation and the Leukemia is gone. We are praying it stays away for good. And since Heaven is a nurse, they want to be doctors when they grow up. I brag about them every chance I get. Not many people that have gone through what I have can say they are raising doctors.

Speaking of doctors, my dad's doctors are surprised that he is still alive. He is fighting the Cancer. It has spread through his body and confined him to the bed. The doctors say there isn't anything they can do because they expected him to be gone six months ago. But dad continues to fight on. We're hoping and praying that God will give us another miracle. The doctors say this will be his last Christmas, and for the most part, we've accepted and made peace with his passing. We're just happy that we can all be together to celebrate one more Christmas. And he's happy that he got to meet his grandsons and swears he won't leave until he meets his granddaughter.

Mom is well. Loving that she will be a grandmother three times over. She actually wants us to have more kids. We aren't sold in the idea though. The jury is still out on whether there will be more additions. Ray doesn't seem like he will ever stop growing. He's seventeen and has grown three inches. Now, he stands six foot five. I hope he stops growing because his size fifteen shoes aren't cheap. He's also one of the best linebackers in the country. He still has one more year of high school and all the top colleges in the nation want him. He is still undecided about what school to attend. Dad wants him to go to Illinois. I'm pushing for him to become a Wisconsin Badger.

My boys are finally wising up and picking good women to settle down with. Well, two of them. Vito is locking down Queesha and all of her booty. They are supposed to get married next summer. Junior and Julie look happy and they seem to be in it for the long haul. Don't know when they'll marry. Julie is focused on her career. And Mike... He's still Mike but life has changed for my oldest friend. For starters, he had to quit smoking weed. At least for two years because of the probation he got for whooping Big John and getting caught with the gun. He also recently found out he is a father. Turns out he fathered Sapphire's youngest son, Marcel. And Mike is a good dad. Even brings Marcel over the house to hang out with the twins every now and then. Speaking of Sapphire, I haven't heard a peep from her since Heaven knocked her out. And I love it!

Heaven is doing good. Her stomach is getting bigger every day. She can't wait to have our daughter so she can have her body back. I kind of like her pregnant. Everything is bigger and the wet parts are wetter. She is continuing her education at Marquette University. She's enrolled in the nursing program to become a registered nurse. Her dream is to work at a big hospital. Maybe one day her and the twins will work at the same hospital. As for me, I'm good. Happy, healthy, and in love. I'm loving being a father to the twins and a big brother to Ray. I'm still welding and part time motivational speaking. I also recorded a few songs, at the pestering of my mom and Heaven, and I'm shopping around my demo. I've gotten over the stage fright and have done a few talent shows. So far, the biggest act I've done is to open up at Summerfest. If I go on to be a big star, that would be great. If not, that's cool too. My family means more to me than millions of dollars. If I had to choose between having a water fight in the backyard with the kids or rocking out at a concert, my family would win every time. Like I said, I'm happy, healthy, and in love. What more can man want? Oh, and those charges for beating up The Hoe Whisperer got dismissed. The pimp never showed up to court. No victim, no crime, case closed.

Lock Down Publications and Ca$h Presents
Assisted Publishing Packages

BASIC PACKAGE	UPGRADED PACKAGE
$499	$800
Editing	Typing
Cover Design	Editing
Formatting	Cover Design
	Formatting
ADVANCE PACKAGE	**LDP SUPREME PACKAGE**
$1,200	$1,500
Typing	Typing
Editing	Editing
Cover Design	Cover Design
Formatting	Formatting
Copyright registration	Copyright registration
Proofreading	Proofreading
Upload book to Amazon	Set up Amazon account
	Upload book to Amazon
	Advertise on LDP, Amazon and Facebook Page

***Other services available upon request.
Additional charges may apply
Lock Down Publications
P.O. Box 944
Stockbridge, GA 30281-9998
Phone: 470 303-9761

Submission Guideline

Submit the first three chapters of your completed manuscript to ldpsubmissions@gmail.com, subject line: Your book's title. The manuscript must be in a .doc file and sent as an attachment. Document should be in Times New Roman, double spaced and in size 12 font. Also, provide your synopsis and full contact information. If sending multiple submissions, they must each be in a separate email.

Have a story but no way to send it electronically? You can still submit to LDP/Ca$h Presents. Send in the first three chapters, written or typed, of your completed manuscript to:

LDP: Submissions Dept
Po Box 944
Stockbridge, Ga 30281

DO NOT send original manuscript. Must be a duplicate.

Provide your synopsis and a cover letter containing your full contact information.

Thanks for considering LDP and Ca$h Presents.

NEW RELEASES

SOSA GANG 2 by ROMELL TUKES
KINGZ OF THE GAME 7 by PLAYA RAY
SKI MASK MONEY 2 by RENTA
BORN IN THE GRAVE 3 by SELF MADE TAY
LOYALTY IS EVERYTHING 3 by MOLOTTI

Coming Soon from Lock Down Publications/Ca$h Presents

BLOOD OF A BOSS **VI**
SHADOWS OF THE GAME II
TRAP BASTARD II
By Askari
LOYAL TO THE GAME **IV**
By T.J. & Jelissa
TRUE SAVAGE **VIII**
MIDNIGHT CARTEL IV
DOPE BOY MAGIC IV
CITY OF KINGZ III
NIGHTMARE ON SILENT AVE II
THE PLUG OF LIL MEXICO II
CLASSIC CITY II
By Chris Green
BLAST FOR ME **III**
A SAVAGE DOPEBOY III
CUTTHROAT MAFIA III
DUFFLE BAG CARTEL VII
HEARTLESS GOON VI
By Ghost
A HUSTLER'S DECEIT III
KILL ZONE II
BAE BELONGS TO ME III
TIL DEATH II
By Aryanna
KING OF THE TRAP III
By T.J. Edwards
GORILLAZ IN THE BAY V

3X KRAZY III
STRAIGHT BEAST MODE III
De'Kari
KINGPIN KILLAZ IV
STREET KINGS III
PAID IN BLOOD III
CARTEL KILLAZ IV
DOPE GODS III
Hood Rich
SINS OF A HUSTLA II
ASAD
YAYO V
Bred In The Game 2
S. Allen
THE STREETS WILL TALK II
By Yolanda Moore
SON OF A DOPE FIEND III
HEAVEN GOT A GHETTO III
SKI MASK MONEY III
By Renta
LOYALTY AIN'T PROMISED III
By Keith Williams
I'M NOTHING WITHOUT HIS LOVE II
SINS OF A THUG II
TO THE THUG I LOVED BEFORE II
IN A HUSTLER I TRUST II
By Monet Dragun
QUIET MONEY IV
EXTENDED CLIP III
THUG LIFE IV
By Trai'Quan
THE STREETS MADE ME IV
By Larry D. Wright
IF YOU CROSS ME ONCE III
ANGEL V
By Anthony Fields

THE STREETS WILL NEVER CLOSE IV
By K'ajji
HARD AND RUTHLESS III
KILLA KOUNTY IV
By Khufu
MONEY GAME III
By Smoove Dolla
JACK BOYS VS DOPE BOYS IV
A GANGSTA'S QUR'AN V
COKE GIRLZ II
COKE BOYS II
LIFE OF A SAVAGE V
CHI'RAQ GANGSTAS V
SOSA GANG III
BRONX SAVAGES II
BODYMORE KINGPINS II
By Romell Tukes
MURDA WAS THE CASE III
Elijah R. Freeman
AN UNFORESEEN LOVE IV
BABY, I'M WINTERTIME COLD III
By Meesha

QUEEN OF THE ZOO III
By Black Migo
CONFESSIONS OF A JACKBOY III
By Nicholas Lock
KING KILLA II
By Vincent "Vitto" Holloway
BETRAYAL OF A THUG III
By Fre$h
THE MURDER QUEENS III
By Michael Gallon
THE BIRTH OF A GANGSTER III

By Delmont Player
TREAL LOVE II
By Le'Monica Jackson
FOR THE LOVE OF BLOOD III
By Jamel Mitchell
RAN OFF ON DA PLUG II
By Paper Boi Rari
HOOD CONSIGLIERE III
By Keese
PRETTY GIRLS DO NASTY THINGS II
By Nicole Goosby
PROTÉGÉ OF A LEGEND III
LOVE IN THE TRENCHES II
By Corey Robinson
IT'S JUST ME AND YOU II
By Ah'Million
FOREVER GANGSTA III
By Adrian Dulan
GORILLAZ IN THE TRENCHES II
By SayNoMore
THE COCAINE PRINCESS VIII
By King Rio
CRIME BOSS II
Playa Ray
LOYALTY IS EVERYTHING III
Molotti
HERE TODAY GONE TOMORROW II
By Fly Rock
REAL G'S MOVE IN SILENCE II
By Von Diesel
GRIMEY WAYS IV
By Ray Vinci

Available Now

RESTRAINING ORDER **I & II**
By CA$H & Coffee
LOVE KNOWS NO BOUNDARIES **I II & III**
By Coffee
RAISED AS A GOON I, II, III & IV
BRED BY THE SLUMS I, II, III
BLAST FOR ME I & II
ROTTEN TO THE CORE I II III
A BRONX TALE I, II, III
DUFFLE BAG CARTEL I II III IV V VI
HEARTLESS GOON I II III IV V
A SAVAGE DOPEBOY I II
DRUG LORDS I II III
CUTTHROAT MAFIA I II
KING OF THE TRENCHES
By Ghost
LAY IT DOWN **I & II**
LAST OF A DYING BREED I II
BLOOD STAINS OF A SHOTTA I & II III
By Jamaica
LOYAL TO THE GAME I II III
LIFE OF SIN I, II III
By TJ & Jelissa
BLOODY COMMAS I & II
SKI MASK CARTEL I II & III
KING OF NEW YORK I II,III IV V
RISE TO POWER I II III
COKE KINGS I II III IV V
BORN HEARTLESS I II III IV
KING OF THE TRAP I II

By T.J. Edwards
IF LOVING HIM IS WRONG…I & II
LOVE ME EVEN WHEN IT HURTS I II III
By Jelissa
WHEN THE STREETS CLAP BACK I & II III
THE HEART OF A SAVAGE I II III IV
MONEY MAFIA I II
LOYAL TO THE SOIL I II III
By Jibril Williams
A DISTINGUISHED THUG STOLE MY HEART I II
& III
LOVE SHOULDN'T HURT I II III IV
RENEGADE BOYS I II III IV
PAID IN KARMA I II III
SAVAGE STORMS I II III
AN UNFORESEEN LOVE I II III
BABY, I'M WINTERTIME COLD I II
By Meesha
A GANGSTER'S CODE I &, II III
A GANGSTER'S SYN I II III
THE SAVAGE LIFE I II III
CHAINED TO THE STREETS I II III
BLOOD ON THE MONEY I II III
A GANGSTA'S PAIN I II III
By J-Blunt
PUSH IT TO THE LIMIT
By Bre' Hayes
BLOOD OF A BOSS I, II, III, IV, V
SHADOWS OF THE GAME
TRAP BASTARD
By Askari
THE STREETS BLEED MURDER **I, II & III**
THE HEART OF A GANGSTA I II& III
By Jerry Jackson
CUM FOR ME I II III IV V VI VII VIII
An LDP Erotica Collaboration

BRIDE OF A HUSTLA **I II & II**
THE FETTI GIRLS **I, II& III**
CORRUPTED BY A GANGSTA I, II III, IV
BLINDED BY HIS LOVE
THE PRICE YOU PAY FOR LOVE I, II ,III
DOPE GIRL MAGIC I II III
By Destiny Skai
WHEN A GOOD GIRL GOES BAD
By Adrienne
THE COST OF LOYALTY I II III
By Kweli
A GANGSTER'S REVENGE **I II III & IV**
THE BOSS MAN'S DAUGHTERS I II III IV V
A SAVAGE LOVE **I & II**
BAE BELONGS TO ME I II
A HUSTLER'S DECEIT I, II, III
WHAT BAD BITCHES DO I, II, III
SOUL OF A MONSTER I II III
KILL ZONE
A DOPE BOY'S QUEEN I II III
TIL DEATH
By Aryanna
A KINGPIN'S AMBITON
A KINGPIN'S AMBITION **II**
I MURDER FOR THE DOUGH
By Ambitious
TRUE SAVAGE I II III IV V VI VII
DOPE BOY MAGIC I, II, III
MIDNIGHT CARTEL I II III
CITY OF KINGZ I II
NIGHTMARE ON SILENT AVE
THE PLUG OF LIL MEXICO II
CLASSIC CITY
By Chris Green

A DOPEBOY'S PRAYER
By Eddie "Wolf" Lee
THE KING CARTEL **I, II & III**
By Frank Gresham
THESE NIGGAS AIN'T LOYAL **I, II & III**
By Nikki Tee
GANGSTA SHYT **I II &III**
By CATO
THE ULTIMATE BETRAYAL
By Phoenix
Boss'n Up i , ii & Ili
By Royal Nicole
I LOVE YOU TO DEATH
By Destiny J
I RIDE FOR MY HITTA
I STILL RIDE FOR MY HITTA
By Misty Holt
LOVE & CHASIN' PAPER
By Qay Crockett
TO DIE IN VAIN
SINS OF A HUSTLA
By ASAD
BROOKLYN HUSTLAZ
By Boogsy Morina
BROOKLYN ON LOCK I & II
By Sonovia
GANGSTA CITY
By Teddy Duke
A DRUG KING AND HIS DIAMOND I & II III
A DOPEMAN'S RICHES
HER MAN, MINE'S TOO I, II
CASH MONEY HO'S
THE WIFEY I USED TO BE I II
PRETTY GIRLS DO NASTY THINGS
By Nicole Goosby
TRAPHOUSE KING **I II & III**

KINGPIN KILLAZ I II III
STREET KINGS I II
PAID IN BLOOD **I II**
CARTEL KILLAZ I II III
DOPE GODS I II
By Hood Rich
LIPSTICK KILLAH **I, II, III**
CRIME OF PASSION I II & III
FRIEND OR FOE I II III
By Mimi
STEADY MOBBN' **I, II, III**
THE STREETS STAINED MY SOUL I II III
By Marcellus Allen
WHO SHOT YA **I, II, III**
SON OF A DOPE FIEND I II
HEAVEN GOT A GHETTO I II
SKI MASK MONEY I II
Renta
GORILLAZ IN THE BAY **I II III IV**
TEARS OF A GANGSTA I II
3X KRAZY I II
STRAIGHT BEAST MODE I II
DE'KARI
TRIGGADALE I II III
MURDAROBER WAS THE CASE I II
Elijah R. Freeman
GOD BLESS THE TRAPPERS I, II, III
THESE SCANDALOUS STREETS I, II, III
FEAR MY GANGSTA I, II, III IV, V
THESE STREETS DON'T LOVE NOBODY I, II
BURY ME A G I, II, III, IV, V
A GANGSTA'S EMPIRE I, II, III, IV
THE DOPEMAN'S BODYGAURD I II
THE REALEST KILLAZ I II III

THE LAST OF THE OGS I II III
Tranay Adams
THE STREETS ARE CALLING
Duquie Wilson
MARRIED TO A BOSS I II III
By Destiny Skai & Chris Green
KINGZ OF THE GAME I II III IV V VI VII
CRIME BOSS
Playa Ray
SLAUGHTER GANG I II III
RUTHLESS HEART I II III
By Willie Slaughter
FUK SHYT
By Blakk Diamond
DON'T F#CK WITH MY HEART I II
By Linnea
ADDICTED TO THE DRAMA I II III
IN THE ARM OF HIS BOSS II
By Jamila
YAYO I II III IV
A SHOOTER'S AMBITION I II
BRED IN THE GAME
By S. Allen
TRAP GOD I II III
RICH $AVAGE I II III
MONEY IN THE GRAVE I II III
By Martell Troublesome Bolden
FOREVER GANGSTA I II
 GLOCKS ON SATIN SHEETS I II
By Adrian Dulan
TOE TAGZ I II III IV
LEVELS TO THIS SHYT I II
IT'S JUST ME AND YOU
By Ah'Million
KINGPIN DREAMS I II III
RAN OFF ON DA PLUG

By Paper Boi Rari
CONFESSIONS OF A GANGSTA I II III IV
CONFESSIONS OF A JACKBOY I II
By Nicholas Lock
I'M NOTHING WITHOUT HIS LOVE
SINS OF A THUG
TO THE THUG I LOVED BEFORE
A GANGSTA SAVED XMAS
IN A HUSTLER I TRUST
By Monet Dragun
CAUGHT UP IN THE LIFE I II III
THE STREETS NEVER LET GO I II III
By Robert Baptiste
NEW TO THE GAME I II III
MONEY, MURDER & MEMORIES I II III
By Malik D. Rice
LIFE OF A SAVAGE I II III IV
A GANGSTA'S QUR'AN I II III IV
MURDA SEASON I II III
GANGLAND CARTEL I II III
CHI'RAQ GANGSTAS I II III IV
KILLERS ON ELM STREET I II III
JACK BOYZ N DA BRONX I II III
A DOPEBOY'S DREAM I II III
JACK BOYS VS DOPE BOYS I II III
COKE GIRLZ
COKE BOYS
SOSA GANG I II
BRONX SAVAGES
BODYMORE KINGPINS
By Romell Tukes
LOYALTY AIN'T PROMISED I II
By Keith Williams
QUIET MONEY I II III

THUG LIFE I II III
EXTENDED CLIP I II
A GANGSTA'S PARADISE
By Trai'Quan
THE STREETS MADE ME I II III
By Larry D. Wright
THE ULTIMATE SACRIFICE I, II, III, IV, V, VI
KHADIFI
IF YOU CROSS ME ONCE I II
ANGEL I II III IV
IN THE BLINK OF AN EYE
By Anthony Fields
THE LIFE OF A HOOD STAR
By Ca$h & Rashia Wilson
THE STREETS WILL NEVER CLOSE I II III
By K'ajji
CREAM I II III
THE STREETS WILL TALK
By Yolanda Moore
NIGHTMARES OF A HUSTLA I II III
By King Dream
CONCRETE KILLA I II III
VICIOUS LOYALTY I II III
By Kingpen
HARD AND RUTHLESS I II
MOB TOWN 251
THE BILLIONAIRE BENTLEYS I II III
REAL G'S MOVE IN SILENCE
By Von Diesel
GHOST MOB
Stilloan Robinson
MOB TIES I II III IV V VI
SOUL OF A HUSTLER, HEART OF A KILLER I II
GORILLAZ IN THE TRENCHES
By SayNoMore
BODYMORE MURDERLAND I II III

THE BIRTH OF A GANGSTER I II
By Delmont Player
FOR THE LOVE OF A BOSS
By C. D. Blue
MOBBED UP I II III IV
THE BRICK MAN I II III IV V
THE COCAINE PRINCESS I II III IV V VI VII
By King Rio
KILLA KOUNTY I II III IV
By Khufu
MONEY GAME I II
By Smoove Dolla
A GANGSTA'S KARMA I II III
By FLAME
KING OF THE TRENCHES I II III
 by GHOST & TRANAY ADAMS
QUEEN OF THE ZOO I II
By Black Migo
GRIMEY WAYS I II III
By Ray Vinci
XMAS WITH AN ATL SHOOTER
By Ca$h & Destiny Skai
KING KILLA
By Vincent "Vitto" Holloway
BETRAYAL OF A THUG I II
By Fre$h
THE MURDER QUEENS I II
By Michael Gallon
TREAL LOVE
By Le'Monica Jackson
FOR THE LOVE OF BLOOD I II
By Jamel Mitchell
HOOD CONSIGLIERE I II
By Keese

PROTÉGÉ OF A LEGEND I II
LOVE IN THE TRENCHES
By Corey Robinson
BORN IN THE GRAVE I II III
By Self Made Tay
MOAN IN MY MOUTH
By XTASY
TORN BETWEEN A GANGSTER AND A
GENTLEMAN
By J-BLUNT & Miss Kim
LOYALTY IS EVERYTHING I II
Molotti
HERE TODAY GONE TOMORROW
By Fly Rock
PILLOW PRINCESS
By S. Hawkins

BOOKS BY LDP'S CEO, CA$H

TRUST IN NO MAN
TRUST IN NO MAN 2
TRUST IN NO MAN 3
BONDED BY BLOOD
SHORTY GOT A THUG
THUGS CRY
THUGS CRY 2
THUGS CRY 3
TRUST NO BITCH
TRUST NO BITCH 2
TRUST NO BITCH 3
TIL MY CASKET DROPS
RESTRAINING ORDER
RESTRAINING ORDER 2
IN LOVE WITH A CONVICT
LIFE OF A HOOD STAR
XMAS WITH AN ATL SHOOTER